The Making of Amityville Theater

John R Walker

DEDICATION

To Mrs. Walker who very kindly let me follow this dream and of course to all the Indie film makers out there.

CONTENTS

ACKNOWLEDGMENTS

I just want to say Thank you to everybody involved with the making of Amityville 13. From Steve Hardy, Matt Hickinbottom, Neilum Raqia, Debbie Reader, Rhodri Jones, Rrain Prior, Monele LeStrat, Tiana Faires, Mike Reader, Linden Baker, Eva Kok, Hollie Anne Kornik, Kenny Benoit, Jodi Venables Baker,   Amanda Naughton-Gale and everyone else in Neepawa who helped make this film. There's so many wonderful people that helped get this film out.

Also to Rob at Wild Eye Releasing for letting me use their amazing cover art.

1 NEVER MAKE YOUR PASSION PROJECT YOUR FIRST PROJECT

Hello

My name is John R walker and I've been a fan of the Amityville franchise for my whole life. For as long as I remember and to this day I have no idea when it started.

I loved the original film and started reading all the novels.

The whole thing caught my imagination and all I ever wanted was more Amityville films (Be careful what you wish for)

My favourite one was the second one. To this day over 40 years later I still love that film and it's probably my favourite all time horror ever.

I followed the franchise through the 80s and the early 90s and then it started to die. Less books and no films for a while.

Then in the 2000s a not so great remake of **Amityville horror** came out. I was pleased they were looking at the series again but was enjoying the lower budget sequels more and that seemed to it until 2011 when The Asylum film company released "**The Amityville Haunting**"

It was the 10th film with the Amityville title but the difference here was that it wasn't an "official" Amityville film.

Not that I'm sure the other sequels were official anyhow as I remember when part 3 came out on VHS it had a message on the back of the cover stating "This film is not a sequel to **The Amityville** Horror " or "**Amityville 2**"

In fact it wasn't called **Amityville 3** back then, it was called **Amityville 3D** so who knows when the official ones stopped but The **Amityville Haunting** was of interest to me as I was wondering at this point what makes an Amityville film official?

The facts surrounding the murders of six members of Defeo's family on 13th November 1974 are in the public domain plus the name of the town is Amityville so with these facts I figured anyone is within their rights to make a film about Amityville and mention the murders.

Obviously the story contained in the **Amityville Horror** were written by the Lutz family so are copyrighted fiction.

It was a lifetimes ambition to be involved in something with the Amityville name in and I never even imagined as a kid that I could simply make my own.

I had been looking for a project to do for a while now and it was Andy Jones '**Amityville Asylum** that really inspired me. when I saw he'd made not only an Amityville film but that he'd shot it in the UK.

This got me thinking. I was always told never to make your passion project your first project but I couldn't help myself and suddenly I was only thinking about an Amityville project morning, noon and night. I had save about £30,000 that I was happy to use on the project but what I needed next was an angle

I knew I had to make it in the UK so it had to be primarily an interior shoot plus it couldn't be the house as I had no access to the house or a house in the UK that could double for the house.

I thought for months and months and just couldn't get an idea that would stick. The whole possessed item synopsis was great but Id still need access to a house that looked like Amityville to get that idea across but suddenly it hit me.

Amityville is in fact the name of the village. Not the house as the house was called "High Hopes" so it didn't have to be a possessed house but a village that the house stands in.

Now all I had to do was think of what building in the town of Amityville would be the centre of the story.

On my way to work every day I would drive past this old Dudley Palladium that had been closed down for many years.

It even had a large pavement outside the front that looked like it could be an American side walk.

This was where I wanted the new film to take place.

The idea was to shoot all the characters inside the building here in Dudley and then get one character to run around the real Amityville in Long Island, NY with a tiny camera team to cut in between the scenes to make the audience think the whole film was being shot in the USA.

In fact to save even more money, I had the idea that I would do the running around the USA shots and that'll save even more by not taking an actor to the USA as we also would need this character to come into the building and interact with the main artistes.

The one big thing that bugged me about the Amityville franchise was that none of the films actually follow on from each other so I wanted this film to have a little of all the films in.

I made a big error on my assumption that I would be able to hire the empty Palladium building for the shoot so I spent my time breaking the previous Amityville films down.

2 RESEARCH

So I made my next task of breaking down all the basic information of the previous films to try and incorporate as much of them into my film as possible so each film is linked.

I watched each film and wrote down how many people died or what spooky happenings happen in the film to incorporate into mine.

This is a copy of the notes I made

Amityville 3D (1983)

Local Information

Amityville Realty 666-1818
The agents name is Clifford Sanders

Dr Elliot West from the Institute of Physic Research- State University – Long Island

David Coller – Local DA

The Caswells exploited the house with fake happenings

Clifton Stone is a book agent

The house blows up. This is 1983

Spooky happenings
- It's always cold
- Lights floating with voices of the Dead
- Bad Dreams
- Demon in the well
- Flies in the windows
- Furniture moves to block exits
- Photos have bad pixilisation of people the house will kill
- The fact there is a well in the cellar that bubbles
- Mirrors frost up
- Doppelgänger of Susan after she'd died
- freezing temperature in moments

Deaths

1. Saunders by flies
2. Susan by Drowning
3. Elliot in well from Demon
4. Camera woman squashed by door
5. Cameraman dies being thrown across a room
6. Melanie burns to death in a car after the breaks failed

Amityville 4 – The Evil Escapes (1989)

Local Facts

- Lamp sent from Amityville to Mrs Alice Leacock, 274 Ocean View Lane, Dancott, California, 93117
- Kids go to Castlefield College
- Helen Royce in NY phone number is 555- 2341
- For 300 years no-one has lived on that ground (Meaning Amityville) without tragic consequences
- The 1974 murders are mentioned though not by name
- This must take place before Amityville 3 as the house still exists

Spooky happenings

- Flys
- Doors open and slam
- Lights go on and off
- Flying furniture
- Bleeding walls
- Demon lives in the lamp
- Pepper the cat hates the Amityville lamp
- Ghost of dead dad (Frank)
- Arm of dead Frank felt in bed though maybe a dream
- Amityville lamp makes people see the dead
- Parrot ends up in the oven
- Chainsaw comes to life
- Waste disposal comes alive
- Evil speaks with a voice through the telephone
- Telephone melts
- Black slime comes out the taps
- Jessica vandalises room whilst possessed
- Window moves and knocks out girl

✄ Demon possesses little girl

Deaths

1. Helen dies from an infection from the lamp
2. Fred the parrot dies in an oven
3. Plumber drowns in black slime
4. Peggy the Housemaid is strangled by lamp lead

Amityville Curse (1989)

Local facts

✄ Sacred Heart Catholic Church is a local Amityville Church
✄ Long Island Express-way is a major road in the area
✄ Realty 516-2123
✄ Dorrys Bar Grill is a local Country and Western bar
✄ Mention is made of a boy who killed his family but the name is never mentioned
✄ The Character and killer "Frank" is the illegitimate son of the Priest

Spooky Happenings

✄ Drafts without open windows
✄ Voices (Latin?)
✄ Demons in dreams
✄ Dogs attack
✄ House shakes with slamming doors
✄ Books fly off the shelf
✄ Mirrors smash
✄ Bathwater turned blood red
✄ confession booth explodes

Deaths

1. priest by shooting
2. Mrs Moriarty pushed down the stairs
3. Boy mistaken for killer hung himself
4. Bill – Death by Frank
5. Marvin – Death by Frank
6. Frank – Death by Debbie's nail gun and then holy staff

Amityville – It's about time (1992)

Local Facts

- Family live in Burnwood Estates in California
- It's implied that Amityville is pulled down for a redevelopment
- Skull Krusher- This is 89 is a T-shirt worn
- Geelee D'ray (Spelling unknown) owned the killer clock. He was a French 15th Century Necromancer who ran a school for intelligent boys. He was teacher/Minister and inventor and eater of the kids to keep himself young. Nothing more is said or explained about this massive piece of information

Spooky happenings

- Clock from Amityville gets louder nearer 03.00
- Dog barks at clock
- Clock shows the boy the torture room from 15th Century France
- Doppelgänger of Mrs Tetman and dog
- Time Travel. The boys has once sentence into a room and back but it's now hours later
- Black tar or dark blood is in dream
- Jacob is cold and gets angry a lot
- Hedge catches fire
- Time stopped altogether
- Doppelgänger dream Jacob
- Mirror shows fake reflection and drips tar before possession of girl (very much like New Generation)
- Wounds won't heal
- Black tar from tap although this may have been a dream. We never find out
- Phones are dead
- Doors won't open
- Windows seal
- People can't see in but we can see out
- Sound also does not penetrate the doors and windows
- Sister wants incest with brother
- Jacob becomes possessed

Deaths

1. Peaches the dog
2. Mrs Iris Wheeler via Ice cream Van bird!
3. Andy via slime in garage that melts him
4. Leonard by hanging
5. Possessed Lisa electrocuted
6. Possesses Jacob by beating from Andrea
7. Andrea by blowing up the place

Although due to time travel no one dies (Let's forget that part)

Amityville – A new Generation (1993)

Local facts

- Franklin I. Bronner takes the place of Defeo and the killings are now about 1966
- Bronner was born Oct 23rd 1949 and died November 11th 1993 which is during the movie time.
- He was 17 when he murdered 4 members of his family by shooting at the dinner table
- Bronner was sent to Dannamora State Hospital Cell 207 in the West Wing and released 17 years later
- His son is Keyes Terry
- Cops came from Psycho Pathology Department

Spooky Happenings

- Photos look like demon faces
- The dead walk or is it another doppelgänger?
- Went inside the Mirror from Amityville
- The mirror is alive as it was from the house and saw the killings

Deaths

1. Suki Boyfriend by mirror showing things that didn't happen and then boyfriend falls into window
2. Suki by Hanging as rope puts itself there
3. Tramp (Franklin I Bronner) unknown
4. Dick (Landlord)... I've forgotten

Amityville Dollhouse (1996)

Local Facts

- Newspaper suggests that "Family burn in house fire- Deranged Father Prime Suspect"
- The house in question is Amityville. The fireplace remained and a new house was built on the site
- Todds parents also died in a house fire but we are never told if this was the Amityville fire
- New house built by Bill martin (Does he own a firm with the same name?)

Spooky happenings
- Nose bleeds for no reason
- The Dollhouse contains the Amityville evil
- Dollhouse is alive and lights its own fires.
- The real house is hot and the fire also lights itself
- Little girl speaks through the fire place... It's a dream
- Car moves itself and squashes bike
- Cooker fire erupts
- Toy spider becomes a real spider
- dollhouse makes people faint
- Dollhouse emulates the real house it occupies
- Giant mouse appears under the bed when real mouse enters dollhouse
- Evil Ghost zombie of dead dad
- Incestuous thoughts of step son.
- Dead insect comes alive and enters Todds head
- Dreams of demons and torture
- House makes Lynda catch fire
- Things move and explode if witchcraft is used to destroy evil
- Insects grow inside dolls
- House makes car start and fumes to kill owners
- Inverted crosses appear inside house
- Real fireplace happens to be a portal into Amityville hell world dimension full of demons but when you open the door you are only actually upstairs in the real world

Deaths

1. Tobias by demons
2. Lynda by fire (we assume she died)

Amityville Haunting (2010)

Local facts

- Local Coroner is Frank R Mackie
- D.Williams is the local Judge
- Footage of the family compiled by Geoff Meed and edited by Cody Peck
- John Matthews dies in the house (about 8 years old)
- In 1998 a letter came out that Ronnie Defeo didn't kill his family but his sister did it.

Spooky Happenings

- Noises in the house
- Doors slam
- Lights flicker
- Camera flickers
- Dark human shapes
- Things move on their own
- Things happens at 03.15
- Flies
- Footprints appear
- Ghosts

Deaths

1. 4 Kids died in the house in 2007
2. Reality lady had an Aneurysm and died on driveway
3. Delivery man fell down stairs
4. Dad's friend died by electrical wire
5. Sister Lori was possessed and exploded
6. Mum Virginia was sucked away and died of 3rd degree burns
7. Brother Tyler died by a Ghost and loss of blood
8. Dad (Douglas Benson) died by being knifed by youngest daughter in the heart

<u>Amityville Asylum (2013)</u>

1. Book title in film – High hope and Broken dreams by Doctor Elliot Mixter

I think that's as far as I got as I cant find any more notes.

I also spent along time going through real books on the history of Amityville to get some facts I could incorporate into the film. I did far more research than possibly needed and Id already read all the fiction novels over the years.

I am no writer. I know I'm no writer but I knew a man who could so I went to my friend Steve Hardy with a crazy long synopsis plus I kept feeding him more and information to incorporate into the films.
I was overloading him. I kept on throwing stuff to poor Steve to add to the script.

3 SYNOPSIS

American Playhouse synopsis

Fawn Harriman had a sister when she was a lot younger. The sister died when she was about 11 years old. What Fawn didn't know was that her sister was a sacrifice for a devil worshipping cult that her parents were a part of. (She had been the first born)

Her parents had lived in Amityville all their lives but let after the sister had been killed. The family then moved away from the town 20 miles up North to another Long Island town and left the Theatre they had owned. It had already started to fall into ruin.

Fawn then grew up in this other town up North and made friends as if she'd always lived here. She had a great childhood but her parents were kind of over protective.

Her parents died in a freak accident 6 months ago. It seems besides the local assets she had been left an old Theatre down south in a small Village set in the town of Babylon, Suffolk County, Long Island NY called Amityville.

The starts with Ed Clayton leaving his house, getting into his car, driving down the highway to Amityville and to the old Theatre (It was called the Hippodrome – This is because you can still read this on the building)

Ed goes into the building for a survey and dies.

Titles. I'd LOVE a rock song that simply tells the story of Eds travel to Amityville where he met his demise (Don't ask me why)

First flash back – Title saying 4 months ago –
This is an interior of an office.

Dorothy Felix (Lesley) is in the office sitting across from Fawn and she is explaining the deeds to the house and the like and that her relatives will be looking after her and she has also a plot of land in the tiny town of Amityville with an old closed down Playhouse that in recent times had played host to a bingo hall until it was eventually closed.
She suggests Fawn sells it, Fawn tells her she'd like to send a surveyor out to see it and she'd like to maybe do it up?

During this conversation Dorothy is slightly distracted by a fly and after the conversation is bitten by it on the arm. She squats it.

(This needs to be a half day shoot in London as this is cheaper than bringing Lesley to us)

Present day

Cutaways of town and then we see Fawn is at the front of the Theatre looking up next to her partner Kyle.

"I can't believe that surveyor never came back to me" "Lucky you never paid him first"
They discuss the only way in is through the old Stage door as all the other doors and windows are blocked up to keep vagrants out. (Dudley Hippodrome)

They go around the back and open the door. (Back of Town hall in Wednesbury)
We go inside and the rest of the gang turn up (except Wendy)

Everyone is a little excited about spending the night in the old building except Fawn who is still a little forlorn (Did I spell that right?)

This is where we introduce Fawn, Kyle, Jevon, Matt and Indy to the audience.

Someone mentions her teacher at school "Yes, Mr Stewart has been really good to me, he's an old friend of the family"
"Are you sure he's not just trying to get in your underwear?"
"No, no, it's not like that. I think he's gay anyway"

Flashback to Long Island High School. (Dudley College)

Mr Stewart (Yes that's me with my glasses on doing either a bad American accent or being a British teacher)
The bell goes, the class run off and Mr Stewart asks Fawn to stay.

"Hey, how are you doing? How are you getting on with your Auntie?"
"Good, they're great."
"I hear you own a theatre?"
"Yeah, crazy huh?, we're going to visit it this weekend"

"We?"

"Yeah, the guys are coming"

"well you be careful" "You know I'm only a phone call away. Tell you what, I'll do some homework on the history of the place (Walker does in fact decide to visit the place and goes to the local library..I'm writing this to remind myself he needs to do this to show off local locations)

"

Current

The team check they've got all they need to spend the night, sleeping bags etc. It's already getting late so they decide to do a quick tour. They separate.

This is now spooky film territory. The mood is slow and eerie.

We see someone wipe the camera.

There's someone in the building.

The teams are Fawn and Kyle

Jevon and on his own "I'm not scared"

Matt and Indy

The intruder who scares the shit out of Jevon is Wendy

Intro Wendy and she chats to Jevon whilst the others walk about

Someone else wipes the screen. Maybe it wasn't Wendy we saw earlier

Everyone finally meets back up at the camp and Wendy is introduced to the rest of the team. She's not made welcome and we already don't trust her.

They decide to get an Ouija Board out. It's seems fun until it moves on it's own.

Meanwhile Mr Stewart is finding lots of info out. He's just found out about the Defeo murders (Wednesbury Library) but wants more info. The librarian informs him he will get more info if he goes to the town.

He doesn't want to at first but seems to be finding out more in regard to the history of the town and the Native American burials there.

Back to the group they all settle down. Wendy grabs her overnight gear. She's been staying here. The thing is I think Wendy is on the run from something? She knows far more than she's letting us know.

The theatre used to be where a local group had to sacrifice someone every year or the demon under the town will kill 6 people himself. The audience have yet to learn this and Mr Stewart will find this out when he comes to town.

The team in the theatre are still chatting and someone asks about Fawns parents. We see a flashback of her at home with her parents. It's all very happy families (American food products needed. No plugs can be seen, wooden floor in house and this needs to be the other half day shoot in London with Cheryl and Spencer)

Back to present

Someone is watching the group.

Jevon gets up in the night for a wee. He goes in search of somewhere to go and is killed off

Mr Stewart is getting so worried with the info he's finding out that he travels that night to Amityville.
The library is closed so he gets a Motel

The next day no one can find Jevon so decide to search for him

It's still early and it's dark anyhow due to the lack of windows

Mr Stewart has been on the computer all night and is so jolly tired.

He goes to the library (It's open on Sundays!) and starts to read more info he's found in a book

The search inside the theatre goes on.

Fawn is in the run down old playhouse stage area, it's dark and dirty but as we start to see light shine on her. She turns and suddenly we're in a new location.
A nice bright new clean stage area with people acting on stage. We see the

audience. They're all watching the play and laughing without taking any notice of Fawn who is near the stage at the front.

Suddenly all the laughter/ acting goes dead quiet. Fawn looks at the audience. We see just one audience member turn her head from facing the front and she stares right at Fawn. She screams (A little body snatcher style) and the others all stop looking forwards and they all turn to her and point. The actors on stage all do the same. People start walking towards her from the doors

Meanwhile Mr Stewart has fallen asleep in the library. He thinks he wakes up and runs toward the playhouse (In American location)

Just when you think the audience have got fawn, he appears from around the corner, they run from the scary audience. The music is loud, the extras are making lots of loud groaning noises.

She wakes up. It's dead quiet and still dark. She had been unconscious and is back in the dark old room....

Mr Stewart also wakes up and plans to go straight to the playhouse. The demon will stop him any way he can

Kyle is with Fawn "Are you Okay?" he was with her all along. "You just passed out"

Mr Stewart tries to get to the playhouse. He runs out of the library taking his evidence with him. He knows now the truth about the place and he's figured out the clan.

He runs out past ocean Avenue (Location running shoot) and gets to the playhouse. He knocks and shouts from the front and has been trying to ring but it's just not connecting

He runs around the back calling and still trying to phone. The door is sealed tight

Scene inside relates to Matt and Indy....???

Meanwhile back outside Mr Stewart runs to the town Hall, up the steps (On location) up the stairs (It can no longer be a Sunday) and inside (Back into Dudley at the building by the Mosque?) to see the Mayor (Can we ask Darren Nessbit? And then office location need to be near him)

The Major is angry at the intrusion but Stewart get the evidence out and shows him. Shows him that 6 people are being killed each year by some demon that lives in the town. That Amityville was once the home of Native Americans where they buried their dead and kept the insane. That he thinks there is a clan that kills people to feed the souls to the demon.

The Major presses a button under the table. Someone comes in and knocks Stewart out.

Meanwhile back inside the Playhouse. Jevon is dead but a Doppelgänger is meeting Fawn and Kyle and doing something naughty (I haven't thought this part through)

Stewart wakes up. Tied up. The Major confesses to being a part of the clan. Killing families first born to try and feed the demon so that "One death rather than 6" but it isn't working

We think he's going to kill Stewart after the whole confession thing. Gets a gun out. Shoots the one who knocked Stewart out and then aims at Stewart. Shoots himself

Back in the playhouse...........................

I'm not sure if I wrote any more but that's as far as the notes go.

The synopsis talks of Lesley playing Dorothy Felix and the Lesley it speaks of is **Village of the Damned** and **Elephant man** actress Lesley Scoble.
I really wanted her in the film.

So.
With a horribly long synopsis given to poor Steve, I then set to work on props , locations and casting.
So March 2014 and we advertised locally for the six main characters. I had heard there's a big budget Amityville lost footage film out in January next year but that hadn't put me off.

But all this changed when my Director of Photography went to Canada to shoot a family wedding. Before we knew it we were changing the whole location to Canada to double for the USA

I kept a diary of most of this process and have included it here. It contains notes from pre and post production

Sunday 5th April 2014 — Casting for Amityville Playhouse

I had advertised for the 6 main teenagers across Facebook. I'm really trying to keep this local so I kept away from the main actors websites. A good few people got in touch and also I had been put in touch with some chap who was interested in coming aboard but behind the scenes. His name was James and I would be meeting him on the casting day. I sent him a script and contacted all the casting applicants enclosing the first part of the script for them and a scene to practice for the casting.

I set up the office in the Old Post office in Wednesbury. It was where we had filmed Dead time so long ago.

Steve the writer turned up too.

I was surprised by those that didn't turn up on the day but the turn was good and I was able to find 3 of the 6 main characters. I was dreading phoning those who hadn't got the roles.

Now though with only a few weeks to go prior to filming I still need 3 actors just all the locations.

The main location was Dudley Hippodrome but with asbestos found in there I would never get in and so my back up a Bingo hall in Wednesbury but a few weeks back some kids had

broke in and burnt it inside! I wasn't sure what to do next.

James turned up and we got along great. He loves the genre and I can feel he'll be a big help in the project.

I spent the next morning contacting American firms for empty packaging/cans and newspapers but I don't think any will agree to helping. Not on my budget

Wednesday 9th April 2014

I spent the day looking for locations. I found a brilliant one for the corridors called the Royal Hospital. It's Dudley based and empty.

I went to see the security who gave me the details of the chap who runs the place but I telephoned a few times and got no reply.

I then went to the Dudley council to find the chap who looks after the building so I could try the Hippodrome again. I got a name. I e mailed but have heard nothing back.

Still 3 actors and all locations short!! I wish I had help!

Tuesday 15th April 2014

Meanwhile My DP (Director of Photography) had gone to Canada for a week or so to see some family but whilst he was there he sent me some photos of the town and said we could shoot there instead of Long Island as it'll be cheaper.

Oh yes, I'd forgotten to mention. The plan with my cheap Amityville film was to shoot all interior stuff in the UK and do some guerrilla filming in the USA in the real Amityville.

To save even more money, I was playing the role of a teacher that just runs around the town as an excuse to show off locations and cut it with the UK stuff.

But Matt had this idea that we shoot the whole thing over the pond and use Canada as the USA.

The more we talked, the more I thought we could shoot the whole movie there. He said his family would like us there and before we knew it he was interviewed by the local press in Canada and they all wanted us there in the small but wonderful town of Neepawa.

He found me a Line Producer and we set to work starting pre production for Canada. The plan is to shoot it at the end of September or early October.

Excited is an understatement as we were now going to shoot my first film in another country.

BUT my next job was to tell the UK cast as I'm recasting everyone and the only UK shot scene will now be in the Mayors office.

Tuesday 20th May 2014 – Amityville Playhouse/Theater

Meanwhile in the Amityville world, I'd made my first Fake book for the film and ordered 3 magnets for the local cars. (The plan is to stick Amityville company magnets on cars to pretend we are really there)

I now had a price for the hire of the theatre. Things were moving forward. And things were getting expensive.

My new line producer in Canada "Deb" was having questions thrown at her left. right and centre. I just want to get on with the casting.

I had been looking forward to my role in Tony Jopias new film this year but now he had a great budget so I had been replaced with real actors. I went from being asked to audition for 2 main roles to auditioning for a one day cameo as a shop keeper! I guess it's best for the project and exactly what I had done with my UK cast so absolutely no hard feelings.

Sunday 22nd June 2014 — Amityville Playhouse/Theater

It had been a crazy weekend. I had finally booked the tickets for Canada from 7th September for 2 weeks. This weekend also had my line Producer whom I've yet to meet do an amazing job of casting in Canada for me. My lovely Auntie had paid for a Clapper board for the film. £180.

Shockingly high price but I can't wait for it to turn up. I had still yet to break the schedule down so that's my next task.

Today I finally met many of the cast members via Skype. But so much has happened in the last few weeks

My wife is having a baby in February but she'll only be 20 weeks when we fly and I'm told that's fine.

Also. I have been talking to a distributor. It was the one I wanted. Not a well-known one but one that gets their films in every shop and I am more interested in distribution than I am money for this movie.

He liked the script and has asked if I'm able to hand the whole finished product in for an April release. I'd said no at first but it looks like we can do it.

He was talking a USA and Canadian release too. I'm not helped by the big Amityville Hollywood movie that is out in January so he wants to capitalise on it.

I'm still one actor short in Canada and I still don't have a mayor for the UK scenes. I'm being assured not to worry about Canada. Debbie, my line producer has been so fantastic.

So. now I've been introduced to Skype. I went to Matt Hickinbottoms house and spent an hour talking to everyone. It's one month today we start shooting.

Lots of my props have turned up over there.

Sunday 17" August 2014— Amityville Playhouse/Theater

Today I finally met many of the cast members via Skype. But so much has happened in the last few weeks

My wife is having a baby in February but she'll only be 20 weeks when we fly and I'm told that's fine.

Also. I have been talking to a distributor. It was the one I wanted. Not a well-known one but one that gets their films in every shop and I am more interested in distribution than I am money for this movie.

He liked the script and has asked if I'm able to hand the whole finished product in for an April release. I'd said no at first but it looks like we can do it.

He was talking a USA and Canadian release too. I'm not helped by the big Amityville Hollywood movie that is out in January so he wants to capitalise on it.

I'm still one actor short in Canada and I still don't have a mayor for the UK scenes. I'm being assured not to worry about Canada. Debbie, my line producer has been so fantastic.

So. now I've been introduced to Skype. I went to Matt Hickinbottoms house and spent an hour talking to everyone. It's one month today we start shooting.

Lots of my props have turned up over there.

Tuesday 26th August 2014 – Amityville Playhouse/Theater

It's 3 weeks until we fly to Canada though and I am only one cast member short. Everything else seems to be on track.

The other big budget Amityville film out next year just changed their name to "Amityville, The awakening".

The distribution company have already said they'd like to change my title.

Wednesday 17th September 2014 — Amityville Playhouse/Theater

Considering the plane wasn't due until 13.10, we still had to get up at 5.30am. I had packed the night before but most of my luggage were props for the film and costume for my own character.

Matt (Hickinbottom) arrived at the house at 7.30 and we went to Heathrow Airport. we parked up and met up with my Special effects man for this job Rhodri Jones. I know Rhod but this was the first he'd met my wife and Matt.

We all jumped onto the first flight. Heathrow to Toronto. It was 7 and half hours.

At Toronto I was worried everyone would be bored as we would have 2 hours wait prior to the next flight.

We stood in customs. Neilum and I went through together. The chap asked us what we were doing in Canada. We told him about the film and he was happy enough, we went through. Matt also went through with no problems.

Finally Rhodri went to a different customs chap. Oh dear. He was taken away for further
questioning.

The remaining 3 of us retrieved our luggage. We picked up Rhods and waited.

Finally I saw him coming out the door towards us. I though all was Okay. Alas no. The customs man he'd been sent to see now wanted to see me!!

I brought my file with me. Inside my file was the script/contact details! addresses! receipts!
insurance details [for us and the liability insurance! schedule and many other things.

He was a seriously stern fellow. He wanted to see our visas. I told him we'd checked and as there was no payment being made to us we didn't need visas. We had explained the situation on the telephone to check all this prior to travelling and were told we would be okay. He said it was up to him to decide whether we did or not.

He wasn't a happy man. He asked about the film, the cast and the like so I simply gave him my file full.

He then wanted my passport. I told him my wife had it. "Where was she?" Well I told him she was outside with Matt waiting for me.

So then we ALL got called back in.

The conversation did go on for a while but we were then sent off to wait in a waiting area to see if we would be allowed in the country. He had made it clear he didn't think we would be allowed in.

It was quite a tense 30 minute wait whilst he went through my stuff A group of people went to see him. I tried to remain positive but the thought of coming home so soon was unbearable after so long organising this venture,

Finally we were called back over. This time his manner was different. He was much nicer and he simply said because I had all the information in the file, then all was well and let us through.

Earlier Matt had taken the Michael because I had a file full of so much paperwork. Thank goodness I had it.

We just made the next flight. 2 and half hours to Winnipeg

There I finally met our amazing Line producer. The woman of which none of this would have been possible. She'd driven 120 miles to the airport to pick us up and now had to drive us back.

Tired Tired Tired

Thursday 18th September 2014 — Amityville Playhouse/Theater

I woke up early — All my props I'd sent direct were here. I sorted through them. It wasn't long before Deb (Our line producer) took us to a chicken diner to look at the location. It was fantastic so we've booked it.

The morning was also spent looking around the theatre and blocking scenes.

We then met up with all the cast to do a full cast read through. It was kind of weird meeting everyone in real life and seeing them play the roles. It was such a special moment.

It was so fantastic to see and hear everyone. Time went on and we suddenly realised it's time to do the first scene

Oh my Lord, this was really happening. We were shooting a film in Canada!

How scary to suddenly have to film something so soon after meeting everyone. I

think expectations were high and it was great how no one knew us but all went out of their way to help

We were filming at a local school so we went over to look at it, meet the extras and look around the place. They even had the classroom prepared for us.

It was weird walking through a Canadian school — Rhodri and I got very excited by the yellow buses — to be fair we also got very excited by the Garbage trucks.

I added a new section to the first scene — I had a few young actors in so I wanted to give a few people some lines.

It didn't really work out so I cut the scene but I did try.

Then we got on with the actual scene. It was supposed to be in Dannarmora in NY so we put some posters up and some flags. I was playing the teacher still.

I didn't really need to play the role but it was written for me as we were going to shoot my stuff guerrilla style initially but there was no need now and I wasn't very good. Unlike the young lady who played Fawn was so utterly amazing. She's 14 years old and fantastic. The

scene took 3 hours to complete so we wrapped and finally had a big "get to know each other" Barbecue.

Friday 19" September 2014 — Amityville Playhouse/Theater

I had 10 scenes to get through today — They are at the very start of the film. It was about a chap called 'Ed Clayton' who has to pop to the Theatre for the pre title. The actor arrived at the house at 9.00 and the first shot was him coming out of the house and getting into his car.

I had a magnet sign for a company I'd made up placed onto the car. We also had to change his number plate to a NY plate. The DP had brought this prop along and I didn't really expect to use it as there were never too many outside scenes. By the time we'd finished, I wish I'd brought 30 with me.

Most of the morning was then spent driving around locally and shooting shots of the cars (and placing Lawn signs into several lawns.. we even asked some people if they'd mind)

The weather suddenly turned into a heavy downpour.

I wasn't worried about the change to start with as it seemed pretty cool that the weather was getting worse the closer this character got to the theatre. Unfortunately , when we finally got there, the theatre was basked in sunshine!

It came back out with a vengeance and dried the ground, the buildings and the cars. Continuity was wrecked. A lot of the driving will now have to be cut form the film. That was where we were going to put the titles.

It took an hour or so to dress the theatre as the exterior of Amityville Playhouse.

We had to take note of all the lettering on the side of the building as it was used to advertise the film they were actually showing this weekend. We changed it to a film called 'Valley of the Demons' as this was Rhodri's yet to be finished film.

Beside the crazy Canadian weather change. the other issue was the smoke machine. It had died prior to us picking it up and we had to do the scene without.

Our actor did a great job of creeping around until his poor untimely death.

The whole day took much longer than expected but somehow we did manage to fit everything in and so we were ready to take on the next day!

Saturday 20th September 2014 — Amityville Playhouse /Theater

We were currently one scene ahead — I was worried that today as we had already filmed the school scene ahead of schedule and we were in a good position that everyone would want to slow down but I had to keep us ahead.

Matt had been editing what we had shot so far in a rough edit so we could see the quality. It looked pretty good. It's just a shame I couldn't say the same about Matt.. He'd been bitten like mad by the mosquitoes during the opening shots of the film from the garden.

They must have taken a fancy to him as no one else had been bit and poor Matt had 100's of sores.

He'd also been up half the night editing.

We had the first scene of the day in a local office. It's a Cultural Arts Centre and not only had they been kind enough to let us film there but they had let me send all my props and mail to their address over the last several months and let us use some of the equipment they had for our filming.

The scene was pretty straight forward with Fawn talking to her lawyer and getting the keys the Theatre. It took a few hours but we got what we wanted.

Whilst we were there in the building we also made a special happy birthday video for our writer who'd turned 50 today!

At this point everyone stopped for lunch — I still had to keep the momentum going so I just took Matt, dressed up as Mr Stewart and did a few driving scenes to complete the scenes where he drives across town to Amityville. I found a house I liked the look of so I knocked on the door to see if they wouldn't mind me filming myself coming out of the door and down the drive.

We had already had some local press on the internet and most people in town knew who we were SO she had seen this and agreed.. It was so brilliant. I've never seen such friendliness as this town.

The next scene also relied on the generosity of nice people as we got the use of a local diner for free.

Seriously its embarrassing how we go out of the country to a town where nobody knows us and everyone is so wonderful, friendly and helpful.

I loved the diner scene. I'd also wanted to hear Rhodri's welsh accent in the film so we wrote him in as the waiter. complete with hairnet!

1t was a Fun moment and the first time that the others in the crew had disagreed with something I was doing. They felt the comedy wasn't needed but I wanted it and it's there. You tell me what you think. (To be fair the internet have **very** much told me what they think of the whole film)

A girl had been in contact prior to us coming to Canada and said she was a big Amityville fan so we had our first extra! She sat in as a local security firm employee.

The diner scene also ended up going really smooth. I still hadn't quite decided in which order the scenes at the beginning of the film would be in and I was fast running out of time if I wanted any changes.

We actually finished the day still with one scene ahead.

Sunday 21st September 2014 — Amityville Playhouse/Theater

I was looking forward to today as it wasn't many scenes. They were just scenes with Mr Stewart (That's me) running around from place to place.

The First scene was as he just got to Amityville and drove straight to the library it's closed.

We set this scene up but heard a train in the distance. The trains here are miles long. Rhodri was just putting up a prop poster on the library door whilst Matt and I were setting up the shot but we knew we wanted this train shot so we all jumped back into the car. I drove as fast as I could to the rail crossing. Unfortunately we were too late and we arrived just as the last carriage was gone.

Disappointed we drove back to our library location and carried on filming those shots.

After lunch we had planned to film Mr Stewart having a dream whilst walking down the street (a scene I eventually cut) but we heard a train out in the distance again. We were far more prepared this time. With no time to waste we drove to another more out the way crossing. I don't know how we did it but we arrived before the train.

We stopped the car- set the camera up and shot the hell out of this scene. It was Mr Stewart in his car waiting at the crossing. It's so he can remember a UK pub scene that we.

I haven't exaggerated the length of these trains. It took a full 15 minutes to go past. We got loads of footage.

We decided to pop to the local motel to shoot Mr Stewart driving in. It would have been a quick scene but Danny, a South Korean chap who runs the Motel was so so nice to us that we asked if he would like to be in the film.

We couldn't believe he said yes

He was amazing. You don't want to go to Amityville!" - I think he has to be our trailer.

He then let us use a room to film in. All free of charge and to cap it off he offered us drinks. Such a nice guy. This town is bloody amazing!

Monday 22nd September 2014 - Amityville Playhouse/Theater

So – Today was the first day of the actual theatre scenes. We have 10 days in the depths of the theatre.

It starts on the outside in the street with the 2 main characters looking up and the theatre looking back down at them

In fact Matt and I started the day by popping back to the motel at 0730 to get a few shots of Stewart leaving the premises early in the morning.

I then got changed and we rushed to the theatre where the crew were setting the exteriors up.

Rhodri was organising it and seemed to be in his element.

But 0800 came and we still had no sign of one of our main actors. (This was a budget shoot and so no one was picked up)

We phoned him, checked his house, the place we were staying, the school. He was nowhere and not answering his telephone.

An hour passed and I was worried he'd dropped out. Where was I going to get a replacement so late in the day?

Finally he arrived. It turned out Id sent him the wrong information.

So the morning was spent getting the 2 main characters into the theatre.

For such a quiet town, it did start to get unusually busy. There were cars, pedestrians, Rubbish trucks and workers and all making so much noise on what had been a really quiet street

Finally we managed to complete the outside shoot and the other actors turned up. We had to work as fast as we could as the light was changing drastically as the morning went on.

Lunch was set up in the green room by our host and Line producer Debbie. She made everything possible. I still couldn't quite believe we're filming a film in Canada

We shot inside for the rest of the day and these scenes were the introductions of the remaining characters.

The day went so well and everyone loved it.

Tuesday 23rd September 2014 – Amityville Playhouse/Theater

I was a tad annoyed with myself for being ten minutes late to my own set. Were working 8 til 8 or until wrap whichever is sooner.

Everyone was waiting outside the theatre. We got excited by seeing the Fire Hydrant being flushed outside the theatre. The Canadians had no idea we didn't have them in the UK.

We went inside and read through today's scenes. We went over it and over it to try and get the emotion

The guys have worked so hard on this and they have so much to remember. It's not just dialogue, its where to stand, reactions, movement and these guys were not trained actors and they were brilliant.

We shot the scene where the characters find their rooms for the first time and because we were ahead of schedule, we managed to get another scene in from later in the week. It was my character (Mr Stewart) banging on the door outside.

This did mean moving all the equipment from inside to outside (I'm not sure I mentioned that a local TV station lent us the lights to shoot this)

I also had to run down the whole town whilst matt and the crew were in a moving vehicle shooting from the road

I ran at full pelt down the road. Blimey it nearly killed me. I don't remember the last time I ran like that.

So far everything is on track and I just hope so much we can keep it up like this and complete the film.

There's even a slot free now tomorrow that I was going to shoot in the UK but it would be great if we could do it here.

Wednesday 24th September 2014 -= Amityville playhouse/Theater

The only cast member we hadn't worked with yet on set was Hollie who played a character called Wendy.

I thought our first scene would be simple and we'd complete by 1030 – how wrong could I have been?

The lobby of the theatre took much longer than I expected to both set up and shoot. We blocked it and rehearsed it **_so_** many times until we were happy to shoot.

A young lady called Dianne from the local paper "The Neepawa Banner" came to see us in regard to a photograph going onto the paper tomorrow.

Meanwhile back at set we got the smoke machine out (That we had borrowed from someone local) and smoked the theatre up. We then turned over and… the fire alarms went off.

Oh dear, we didn't know what to do to turn them off and the fear of local fire dept coming here to find it was a false alarm. An alarm that we have no idea to turn off.

We looked everywhere for a control panel but couldn't find one that looked like it would turn the alarm off.

So we phoned everyone mentioned on the office wall but no one knew what to do

Strangely enough after 15 minutes of a very loud alarm (We did call the fire brigade but had to leave a message because they were busy) it was Hollie who played Wendy who found a key, she found the alarm box and turned it off.

At this point Id lost my good mood a tad and was getting a little stressed as I was worried we'd get behind schedule but there is no time on shoot to get behind (Why didn't I book extra days to relax and have a holiday?) but al was well and I think I was worrying needlessly

Now, in the street Id spotted a book store that I loved the look of so we squeezed some time in to pop along and see if they'd mind us using it plus whether there would be someone available to play a shopkeeper?

So, again in typical Neepawa style, I went and asked the chap (Jim) if I could ask a few favours. He said Yes to anything even before I managed to get the question out

Then, he said "Who's looking after you?" and we said we were staying at Debbie's so he comes out with 2 dozen eggs for us to eat. I love this town.

Then I popped to the local library. We needed and exterior shot as I planned to shoot inside in a UK library due to the amount of fakes books I didn't want to bring to Canada. And of course when I asked they said yes straight away again. They even invited us to shoot inside but it was neither scheduled and of course the books issue. I wish at this point I had brought them and put more days on the shoot.

The last scene of the day had most the cast in as it was the reaction shots after a girl had fallen from the balcony.

The guys were great and Rhodri did a lovely job of the "ghoul" make-up

Thursday 25th September 2014 – Amityville Playhouse/Theater

I got to the set at 0800 but everyone was running late this morning. I only had 2 actors so we took the time to rehearse and block the scene several times.

Finally the rest of the crew arrived but it wasn't a worry as today was one of the lighter shoot days.

The first scene had the 2 artistes see a third one fall from a balcony to her death.

It was a tough one to shoot as we had a body to fall from above at the correct time and had to keep taking the body back upstairs only to throw it off again and again.

Our main artiste then came in to be made up to play a dead version of herself.

It took a while in make up but Rhodri did a great job and the scene only took 15 minutes to shoot but twice as long was spent for the crew to have our photos with her.

At lunchtime the local paper came in and took several photos. Ewe had made the front page a week ago before we came to town but not this time. Some nice big photos though.

I wanted to change location for the next scene but we were against the clock and we had to do a rat scene without a real rat so we went off to shoot hat and then came back to the theatre to shoot some shots of Don (A chap who dies at the beginning) as a zombie. He wasn't available to us when we shoot the end so we were getting the shots in today

He was made into a zombie demon and having these shots done today meant a little less for Rhodri to do next week.

Don looked fabulous. Scary as blighters and we got what we needed from several angles just in case we change the blocking next week. , oh and again we spent 15 minutes taking selfies with him .

We completed his zombie scene and got him cleaned up ready for our first re shoot. We were killing him off again.

The real projectionist for the theatre popped so we took the opportunity to see some of the footage on the big screen.

Friday 26th September 2014 – Amityville Playhouse/Theater

Everyone made to set on time this morning and to be honest I was a tad moody yesterday with the late start and everyone knew how much we had booked in for today.

We felt like a well-oiled machine today.

We started the day doing a read through with the cast. We rehearsed as much as we could. The cast worked so hard and I was so proud of them and I was pushing and pushing but everyone remained so calm. I had so much respect for these young artistes.

We had 3 scenes in the girls bedroom set and then we moved to the chaps bedroom set. They all had pages of dialogue.

I , myself only had a few lines to learn and I hadn't actually learnt them yet.

Even at this late stage I still wasn't sure if I liked the ending of the film and felt it needed something more. I decided to kill Mr Stewart (the character I was playing)

Rhodri had his hands full (Quite literally) as he had to scar up an actors hand. Twice in fact and I wasn't giving him the time he needed but we were starting to fall behind again today and I didn't want to make any scene cuts.

We crammed so much into today and we still had more to do.

We finally got to shoot in a really cool basement. This was supposed to be how Wendy got into the building but unfortunately the smoke machine died on us half way through so that put an end to this sequence as we didn't have a spare and this would need picking up.

Had I mentioned we met the mayor the other day. We cheekily asked if he could shut a road for us. Well some unbelievable news came in today that they're going to close a road for us for 2 hours on Monday to accommodate the filming. Seriously they're closing a flipping road for us! I love Canada!

Imagine if we asked that in the UK.

Saturday 27th September 2014 – Amityville Playhouse/Theater

Tired Tired Tired And it was so tough getting up today but we did get up and make it to the theatre in time to meet all the cast that were already there.

Today they had magically secured us a new smoke machine. Amazing.

We got straight on with the missing scene from yesterday and it was done within the hour.

Next we all sat down and went through the scenes of the day. It was obvious we wouldn't have the space we needed to shoot the Ouija scene in the room we had planned so we found a new location within the theatre and did a rewrite of the scene so it would work within the story.

I have a handmade Ouija board but it was too heavy to bring with me so I had to settle for a shop bought one. This was a mistake as I later found out in post I found out who belonged the copyright but luckily Hasbro were good to me and let me have the rights to use the scene.

The day flew by, it was tough keeping on top of the scenes and getting them in on schedule plus we still had two scenes to shoot before 1900 (It was 1600 now) as they were using the cinema as a real cinema at 1900

One of the scenes was shot at the wings and the young actress who played Fawn broke down in tears on cue every time. She was amazing.

We were packing up and leaving as the real audience were making their way in.

There were so many nice comments from people passing us who knew what we were up to. (That was most people as it was a small town and we'd been in the paper)

Sunday 28th September 2014 – Amityville Playhouse/Theater

So – Today we had to kill Indy. What a shame. I love the fact that in this film we get to kill people and they're still running around as walking dead or zombies or something.

Anyhow we were able to stay ahead of the schedule and each scene seemed to get quicker as we moved the camera around the room to shoot everyone individually.

I also made some cuts today but because *I* wanted them rather than time dictating what we had to lose.

Lots of moving around today and it took a while to set up the lights and the like plus we had to get one of the actors into "dead" make up as we had a scene where we meet "undead" Jevon. Currently it's my favourite scene. How I wish we had the time or money to get special visual effects.

It felt great staying ahead of the schedule and we got to shoot at another location today as we were filming in the Viscount centre. The town had been so generous and I do hope we get to come back and shoot here again someday.

The local TV station had lent us lots of equipment which was easy enough to use but when it came to setting up the stage lights for the theatre, that was a different story and we were using them tomorrow as we have a big scene with lots of extras but it took us hours to figure out

Monday 29th September 2014 – Amityville Playhouse/Theater

I'd been dreading today for so long but at the same time, I'd been so looking forward to two of my favourite scenes.

I'd had the opera scene in my head since before the film was even written.

Matt had written a theme – I heard it about a week before I came here. I loved it.

A relative of his over here in Canada is an Opera singer so I was over the moon when she agreed to be in the film.

She had written some lyrics for the theme and it sounded wonderful.

Wed put an advert out for local people to come and join in the filming About 20 turned up.

I had hoped for more but was told that I should have filmed the scenes with the Extras on Sunday as everybody works in the week.

It didn't matter, we managed to move everyone so it looked like the theatre was full.

It was so weird seeing my vision come to life. When the press turned up to photograph us , it seemed only right to get them in the scene as well.

It was a dream sequence as our lead "Fawn" walks through a now open and live theatre.

It's a 45 seconds sequence but was worth the time and effort that went into it.

No time for lunch today as at 14.00 I had booked another 25 extras for an exterior scene.

The road had been closed (seriously the Mayor had closed the road off for us! I love this town) and I had my Amityville School bus on set – I've never been so excited in my life – My very own Amityville American School bus!

They had got the lettering on the side of a big yellow school bus just for us.

I had cars placed all over the road as it was being kept closed for 2 hours.

The scene never initially had people in it but it's when Stewart comes out of the Mayor's office and runs to the theatre so I included the whole town of Amityville standing there and watching without having to do anything as they're fully aware the demons beneath the Playhouse will do with him as they please.. It was weird to do and I kind of felt silly as I have little to no faith in my own acting capabilities. (and rightly so)

What a day..but it wasn't over just yet, besides working on some crazy short movie for Rhodri with some of the main cast in it called "Next Stop – Amityville" we went back to Debbie's to shoot the Fawn Flashback scene with her parents before their untimely death.

By now it had been over 12 hours since we started the day and we still had several night shots of the Theatre.

Matt and I drove but the banner had fallen down and cars were in the way so we had to wrap early (Early?)

Tuesday 30ᵗʰ September 2014 – Amityville Playhouse/Theater

The penultimate day and somehow we are still on schedule (I know I seem surprised by this but this has been a very tight shoot)

It was Monele's birthday (who plays Fawn) and we got her an Amityville cake. It was a shame the shop spelt Amityville wrong!

I got Rhodri straight to work with 2 dead people (Deadish as one had to be a living dead. There is a difference. Honest) and then we had to update him to a giant exploding boil face.

Whilst we were filming dead girl under the stairs the press turned up again. I had no idea they were coming back so soon but it turned out to be a different newspaper to the last one. This was the Neepawa press.

They said they wanted to outdo the other paper and give us a front page feature plus full page 3.

They wanted candid onset photos rather than set up pictures. They took photos of the exploding boil and later came back to show us the pictures they had taken.

The downside is that it won't be out until week on Wednesday after we've left town but they did promise to send us copies.

I gave them five minutes of spiel for the film so I do hope they do us proud.

Considering I kept pushing Rhodri with the effect and how much time we had, he really did an amazing job.

Wednesday 1ˢᵗ October 2014 – Amityville Playhouse/Theater

This was the final day of shooting here in Canada. We were all so tired (and my poor 6 month pregnant wife had been booming the whole film so she was especially tired)

I set a lot of time aside for today as Rhodri and a lot of make up to do on 3 people.

We had enjoyed shooting the film and something we did just to help push the fact that Wendy was a ghost was to shoot all her scenes with and without her so we could get rid of reflections of her in each room. I thought it was a little too much in your face but nobody's ever actually noticed. We even did her last scene today and made her simply disappear at the end of it.

I had a few scenes myself today but only walking around the building as Mr Stewart.

We did what we could as it took 6 hours to get those 3 people made up to full undead zombies.

At this point, we had re written and changed the ending so many times. To the point that I'm not sure how it'll cut together when we shoot it . Ha and my own acting was not great but it's a little late now!

We wrapped a little early today and all went out to dinner. It was a little melancholy knowing I'll not get to see some of these people again

Saturday 30th November 2014 — Amityville Playhouse/Theater

So I have now booked a location for the Pub scene. Lesley Scoble helped me but the bad news is that Barbara Shelley says she's too ill to film it. I need to replace her ASAP! I'm not changing the date.

Tuesday 16th December 2014— Amityville Playhouse/Theater

So I had to change the date of the Pub scene. This is going to be in the New year. I need to rush as the film needs to be handed in in January! But today at least my final 2 missing scenes were shot.

The first was in Wednesbury local library. It was a quick scene which was lucky as I only had permission to use the location between 07.30 and 09.30. We arrived at 07.30 but to our dismay the place seemed empty. It was locked up tight. 20 minutes later we found that someone was in the building.

She let us in and simply left us to it. The first shot was a wide so the first job was to hide

Christmas. My guest actor this morning was a chap called Andy Tea. Andy has a great talent with accents and voices so I asked if he'd be my librarian. He was great. Really creepy.

We then had to set the desk up. I had to lose all references to Wednesbury library and turn it into an American library in moments as we just didn't have much time . The USA flags and Vote Elliot Saunders signs and banners went up and hid most the stuff.

I had brought several books with me that I had spent months making and getting printed. All fake books about Amityville. Cheekily I also brought my own book along to place on a shelf in the background.

My wife had a small role, I hope her few lines get away with the accent.

All the hooks were fake except for a couple that I had been given permission to use. We rushed the shoot and got pretty much what we wanted. Sometime a small team is best as we had everything back as it was just in time for opening.

2015

Sunday 12th January 2015 —Amityville Playhouse/Theater — Final shoot

So finally . the last day of shooting. Considering I have to hand the whole project in completed, graded, sound mixed, scored and the like in just a few weeks.

The name had been changed by the distributor to the Amityville Legacy but had changed back to "Playhouse". I'd had an concept poster art sent to me and it was a better title for the artists it seemed.

Well, back to today. We were up at 03.30. Getting this pub sorted for this shoot had been a blighter.

There's football on the television this afternoon and most pubs didn't want me in there. I had several people being so kind and working hard to find me somewhere. It turned out that my wife's friend in South London had a local that were happy to let me shoot in. I hadn't wanted to go to South London but it seemed like the only option left with so little time plus the artistes in this scene were all based in that area.

I had had to wait until Christmas and the New year were out the way until any pub would have me.

I picked up Matt (Hickinbottom) and our onset photographer turned up at the house. The 4 of us (My wife the boom op also) drove down to Streatham

Friday 10th April 2015 — Film released on 6 Showcase cinema screens

I was just checking the internet and as usual put my film title in and suddenly up pops several sites to tell me it's on the big screen. This was weird as I wasn't aware it was getting a limited theatrical run.

The nearest place was Derby, where the writer lives so we got in touch and planned to meet up at the cinema at 21.15. The film starts at 21.30.

I was quite late leaving work and it's 45 miles to Derby, let alone on a Friday night but I went home Changed, and rushed as fast as I could to Derby. I knew where the Showcase was as 1 used to have a house near there.

I managed to get there in time. I parked up, ran through the Mall, up 3 flights of stairs but I couldn't see a mention of my film. Was the internet mistaken?. Well the queue was rather long and it was already 21.20 but as luck would have it, another lady sat in a chair and invited people to her queue

"Is Amityville playing here? I enquired

"No" she said

I showed her the screen grab of the site.

Oh' she replied You want the other Showcase about 5 minutes' drive from here

AAAGH' I was never going to make it.

She gave me the address. I ran 3 flights of stairs, through the mall, and up the street to my car.

I put the address in the Sat Nat and drove to the other location.

I'm not sure why I was in a such a hurry, it's not like I don't know the film inside out but I got to the cinema. Steve (Hardy the writer) had bought me a ticket and I ran into the show.

Lucky I was there. That made 3 of us watching the film.

Monday 13th April 2015 — Film released on DVD

So work were really nice and let me start late so I could go out and see my film in the shops.

It's in HMV, Morrisons, Asda, Sainsburys but unfortunately not in Tesco. I bought an Amityville vest for the baby and we went in search of them all. Sainsburys had it in at number 10.

Morrisons at number 12 in the main chart.

The good news was is was being seen.. The bad news was that people were starting to see it as a real film.

I had "The Guardian" do a review on it and "Radio Times"

I mean the Guardian reviewed my £30,000 film as if it was a real film with a real budget. The Guardian!!

Oh..Ouch. I was slaughtered. It was compared to porn acting! They hated the directing, the effects and everything.

The good news is that it was being accepted as real film but a bad one. I don't think most these people had seen a low budget movie before but I read what people had to say and hopefully learnt from it ready for the next film.

Even the Telegraph mentioned it in passing. "With Amityville Playhouse being released this week, here's 10 other films based on true events" it said

And went on to discuss other films

5 A SECTION I WROTE FOR IAN CARROLS' AMITYVILLE MOVIE GUIDE BOOK

<u>Amityville Playhouse/Theatre (2015)</u>
<u>AKA</u> *<u>Amityville 13</u>*
<u>The following was written for a book following the Amityville</u>
<u>films</u>

Isn't it time you gave The Amityville Theater/Playhouse another chance?

Hi, My name is John R walker and I'm a jolly big fan of the Amityville franchise.

It started in the early 80s when I saw **Amityville 2** on VHS. (To this day still my favourite horror film) and back then we had no internet so all I had to carry on my obsession were the novels.

I would search bookshops high and low to find all the books they'd written and in the meantime I would enjoy the first few films over and over on trusty VHS.

In 1986 Lovebug Starski released a comedy single called *"**Amityville, The house on the hill**"*

I always said I wanted to make a cartoon video for this song but it the best I did was draw it up in comic fashion in an exercise book I got from school.

I had tried to find contact details for him and see if I could some sort of involvement in the film but I was unable to find any. He has since passed away

So the obsession carried on and I was so pleased with each new film that came out. *"**Curse**"* *"* *1992-Its about time*" , *"**New Generation**"* and *"**Dollhouse**"* and then the franchise seemed to have come to an end.

A few years later the remake of *"**Horror**"* followed by a very strange film called *"**The Amityville Haunting**"*

It was at this film I came to the realisation that it wasn't part of the official franchise (Maybe the others weren't but it was not noticeable until now) and I realised that "Amityville" is a town name and you can't franchise a town plus the events in the 1970s with Defeo murdering his family are all in public domain as you can't copyright facts (Obviously the event in "Horror" are copyright as they're a work of fiction)

Suddenly I realised this is the film I wanted to make.

A wise person once said to me *"Don't make your dream project first"* I never listened and I never understood why but I guess I do now, although I would have worried, had I of made something else that I'd never get round to making my Amityville film.

My history in the Indie market as 1St AD and second unit director but I had never made my own feature.

I was previously Head of Corporate films at Morrisons Supermarket but features and corporates are very different and had wanted to make own film for years.

 I was finally going to do it..but how?

Well the answer came to me with the next "Unofficial" Amityville film to hit the streets. This was from Cult director Andy Jones.

I bought the *"Asylum"* and realised he'd actually made it in the UK. I now know it is possible and I was going to do the same.

The thing that bothered me most about all 11 films was the fact that they don't fit together in regard to continuity so I made it my first task to break all the films down 1 by 1.

Film 2 took place first, they sold the house to the Lutz s who ran away from it.

It was up for sale in the 3rd one and exploded in the end but before this happened they sold furniture from the house so a lamp, a clock, a dollhouse, a mirror and then the house is destroyed at the end of part 3.

A new house is built on the site for Amityville Dollhouse which again is destroyed so that the Asylum is built on the same site and so on and so forth.

I then broke down the deaths in each film and whether they were spooky deaths and how they happened and number of deaths.

I had compiled a list of who died, where and how.

Finally I bought books on the real history of Amityville (Village) and jotted down fires and deaths

In fact I did TOO MUCH work and tried to fit too much into the film to the point that he main story is lost.

You see the idea was to make an American film in the UK for a very low budget (As I was financing the thing myself)

I got in touch with a writer and we went through the initial idea that the film would be based inside an old theatre. (Simply because there was no access to a house that looked either American or even remotely like the Amityville house plus as the name Amityville is the name of the village and not the house)

By being filmed inside, it meant we could hide the fact it's British. At the same time, the camera operator and I would go to the real town of Amityville in Long Island, New York and shoot some guerrilla shots of me running around.

I was taking the role of the teacher to simply save money on travelling someone else to the US.

So the film was written to be inside a theatre and a few external shots of the teacher to let the audience think we'd shot the whole film in the USA.

I wanted to film in Dudley (In the West Midlands) where there is a large disused Theatre with a large pavement very much like American side walks. I even had a back-up theatre in Wednesbury just in case I couldn't get the use of this one.

We tried to use the one by the zoo in Dudley but Dudley council had no intention of a low budget film going in there. I was given every excuse going to not film in there with the final word being that there is asbestos above all the entrances and exits.

I had tried every angle in regard to them helping local film makers, I said it would be good for the community if we had a film made here and so on but they weren't interested in my project and neither were the "Save the Dudley Hippodrome" group who I thought would be interested in someone helping their cause .

So whilst I was casting in the UK for actors who can do American accents, I tried my back up theatre in Wednesbury. Another closed down cinema but this one had recently been broken into and set fire in the basement thus making it unsafe to go inside

Meanwhile I was still doing my homework on the history of the town and I kept adding more to poor Steve (Hardy – writer) to add to the script in regard to links to the other films and ideas I kept getting.

I was trying to link my film with EVERY Amityville film made before it.

BUT I still had no location in the UK. I tried so many old cinemas, some open, some that were turned into bingo halls but simply could not find a local location to shoot this film in. Was it going to end before it even starts?

Meanwhile my DP popped to Neepawa in Canada to shoot his cousins wedding.

Whilst he was there, he had mentioned I was struggling to find a location to be an American Theatre

Well the next thing you know, he's sending me photos of their local cinema which they were only using two evenings a week.

To cut a long story short, we decided to shoot it in Canada (except for the London scenes, the library and the Mayors office which were all over here in the UK)

The downside here is that I never had the script re written to reflect our new location as this could mean we could get away with a lot more external shots than were used.

The crew consisted of 4 people, which included my pregnant wife who played was the boom operator throughout and the people of Neepawa were the friendliest nicest most helpful town I've ever been too and went out of their way to help get this film made the little to no budget we had.

Anyhow, that's all a story for another day but we shot in the Autumn of 2014 and the film was picked up and released in April 2015.

Another indie Amityville film had a release in February 2015 (**Amityville Death House**) which then made my film the 13th release.

Anyhow here some of the links from Playhouse/Theater to the earlier films

I wasn't sure how much information was accurate but I broke down the other films to incorporate these links I put into the film

Skull Krusher (Rockin since 89)

This can be clearly seen in the poster outside the theatre

In the "*1992 Its about time*" movie, there is a T shirt that one of the mains wears. It is for the band "Skull Krusher"

I couldn't find any evidence that such a band actually existed at the time but there is now a band with that same name. I contacted the band to see if they would like to see their name in the film and although they agreed, they'd got back to me way after we'd wrapped filming.

Dorrys Bar Grill

As seen on several posters.

In the "*Curse*" film they go to a bar but I was never sure if I was correct in the name of the bar but believe it was this. So it's a bar in the film world of Amityville

Opera of Gilles de Rais

The Opera that the ghost sings.

Gilles de Rais is a confessed serial killer of children from the early 1440s and if I'm remembering correctly, he was the demon from "*1992 – It's about time*"

13th November

So the film takes place in the couple of days leading up to and including 13th November 2015 (One major error was that it wasn't actually a Sunday in 2015) but the date is used constantly throughout the film and seen on posters but most importantly it is the date by which 6 people in the village must be sacrificed to the 6 demons trapped in the catacombs below the town to sate their appetites and stop them from destroying the whole population of the town.

The first born of all the villagers is simply sacrificed for the demons and any unwelcome visitors.

People are not allowed to leave the town if born there or they get found and killed (Fawns parents) and their kin brought back to pay the price of leaving.(Fawn)

Defeo killed the 6 members of his family on this date.

Dannemora
You think I picked a random town in upstate New York to start the film to explain the slightly Canadian accents? (That's my excuse as I have no idea of Dannemora accents)
The town has a hospital for clinically insane according to *"A New Generation"* as its where the "Defeo" character (in all but name) was put after killing his family in that particular movie so that's why we start our film there.
In the restaurant scene near the beginning of *"Playhouse"* we can see a lady eating her lunch and on her Tee shirt is "Security - Dannemora state mental hospital for the totally Insane" and outside the restaurant there is a large white car with the words "Dannemora State Hospital #207 West Wing" which is her characters car.
The 207 West wing is where they kept the character in *"A New Generation"*

Amityville Roxy Playhouse sign – 555- 9400
If you look at the telephone number on the top of the theatre it says " For more information contact Amityville Real Estate 555-9400 and this is the same real Estate number used in *"Amityville 2"*
This company can also be seen on the side of one of the cars
Shinnecock Native Americans
The Shinnecock Native Americans that migrated from the Eastern end of Amityville that discovered the demons were a real tribe that lived in that area of Long Island

3.15
At one point in the film when Jevon wakes up early on the Sunday morning, he's asked "what time is it?" by Matt and replies it's just gone 3.00
This is a nod to the original **"Horror"** when everything happened at 3.15
Blue car parked outside theatre at the beginning of the film –
The sign on the side of the car reads "Amityville – Sacred Heart Catholic Church" and this is a reference to the local church in **"Curse"**

Books.
High hopes, Broken Dreams by Dr Elliot Mixter
As shown in the Amityville library, this book is mentioned in **"Asylum"** but never shown until now
Amityville Catacombs of Long Island by Helen Royce and Clifton

Stone

As shown in the Amityville library, this faux book is written by Helen Royce (A character from "**The Evil Escapes**" and Clifton Stone is a book agent named in "**Amityville 2**"

Amityville – A history of Ghosts, Fact or Fiction by Dr Elliot West

As shown in the Amityville library, this faux book is written by Dr Elliot West, a character from "**3D**"

Anyhow I'll stop talking now

The film got a 6 cinema release in the UK, a full national cinema release in the Philippines, a 3D blu ray release in Germany, a full UK DVD release and was in all major retailers including HMV, Sainsburys, Morrisons, Asda and the like and a full USA/Canada release , again in all major retailers like Target and Walmart.

Wild eye currently have the film available worldwide.

I did come back to the Amityville franchise as actor only as I play news reader Peter Sommers in "**Amityville Clownhouse**" (directed by Dustin Ferguson) and the same character returns in the forthcoming films "**Amityville Hex**" (Directed by Tony Newton), "**Amityville in The Hood**" (Directed by Dustin Ferguson) and "**The Amityville Exorcist**" (Directed by Tony Newton)

6 THE FINAL SCRIPT (WRITTEN BY STEVE HARDY)

CLAYTON
Mary, I'm at the Roxy Theatre. Copy of this to go to Mrs. Dorothy Felix of Coopers, Francis & Foster and Miss Harriman. Addresses… (PAUSES TO LISTEN)…Addresses are in the file. (PAUSES AGAIN) Mary, make sure to check out the alarm sensors on the doors and windows. If think a bunch of homeless deadbeats may have broken in and are making the place their pad.

CLAYTON (CONT'D)
Somebody there!? I'm recording all this! (HOLDS UP RECORDER)And I've got a camera. I'll turn it over to the police! Better stop jerking around!

STEWART
Okay, remember you assignments for Monday morning. No excuses, please!

STEWART (CONT'D)
Fawn, can I see you for just a moment?

STEWART (CONT'D)
Yeah, cut it out! Cut it out!

STEWART (CONT'D)
How're you doing?

FAWN
Okay I guess…

STEWART
How're you settling in with your aunt and uncle?

FAWN

Great… I just wish they wouldn't try so hard. A little space would be nice. They're always asking me if I'm okay.

STEWART
Ah!

FAWN
No! I didn't mean it like that! I didn't mean YOU! You're kinda different.

STEWART
I'm gonna assume that's a compliment! Anyway, I hear you now own a theatre?

FAWN
Yeah. Crazy, right? It's over in Amityville. We're going over to take a look this weekend.

STEWART
We?

FAWN
You know, the guys – Kyle and Indy and Kyle's brother. It'll be a kind of sleepover. We'll get pizza and stuff. Tell ghost stories. It'll be kind of fun.

STEWART
Kyle's idea..?

FAWN
(GIGGLES SLIGHTLY) Yeah, I guess…

STEWART
I remember Kyle Blaker back from when he was in my classes. You could have more than things going bump in the night to deal with!

FAWN
Kyle's cool. People have the wrong idea about him.

STEWART
I hope so! I miss your parents, too… Look you know you can call me any time…

FAWN
Thanks.

STEWART
Tell you what, why don't I do some research into your theatre's history? It'll give me something to do over MY weekend. If I find anything interesting out I'll let you know Monday. How's that?

FAWN
Great!

STEWART
By the way, what do you plan to do with your theatre?

FAWN
I don't know… Maybe I'll let YOU know Monday! How's that?

STEWART
Sounds like a plan. Have a great weekend, Fawn!

FAWN
Thanks, Mr. Stewart! You too…

RHODRI
Here you go. Here's a couple of menus to get you started. Drinks? You look thirsty. How about a soda?

FAWN
No thank you.

RHODRI
(TO KYLE)

KYLE
No, I'm good.

RHODRI
Let me tell you about my all-day breakfast specials. They're—

KYLE
(FIRMLY) We're good. We're fine.

RHODRI
Right…

KYLE
(TO FAWN)Did you get 'em?

KYLE
(GRINNING) Did she suspect anything?

FAWN
Suspect WHAT, Kyle? It's my theatre. I don't have to make excuses. Not everyone is as devious as you, you know.

KYLE
So everything's cool..?

FAWN
Yes, everything is 'cool'. (BEAT) One thing's weird though… She said *With your parents gone too'* What did she mean by, *'too'*?

KYLE
Who cares? Bitch is probably shitfaced. (BEAT) Do you wanna buy me lunch, babe?

FAWN
(UNENTHUSIASTICALLY) Yeah, I guess…

KYLE
I wonder if they do chicken-fried steak here..?

DOROTHY
Fawn, honey… This is a large commercial property that your parents were eager to dispose of anyway. I can arrange to sell it for you. You wouldn't even need to be involved. I can do everything for you. It's

within the terms of the will for me to dispose of any of the assets you don't wish to keep.

FAWN
I don't know if I DO want to keep it, Mrs. Felix, but I think I should at least take a look at it.

DOROTHY
Why?

FAWN
I didn't know my dad even HAD a theatre.
DOROTHY
It's been sitting empty for nearly five years.

FAWN
Is it in bad shape?

DOROTHY
Well, it's not exactly falling down but there's been no maintenance done on the building itself for a long time.

FAWN
What would I need to do?

DOROTHY
Well, for starters you'd need to get it inspected before you could make any real decisions as to its future.

FAWN
All I want to do is look it over. You can't stop me from doing that; it IS mine after all!

DOROTHY
(SLIGHTY COOLER) It is not my intention to stop you. I'm merely here to advise you…

FAWN
So can I have the keys..?

DOROTHY reaches for an envelope and takes out a set of keys.

DOROTHY
There's an alarm system. The code is on this piece of paper along with instructions as to how to switch on the power. There are two sets of keys. Would you like me to keep one and arrange for a surveyor?

FAWN
Yes please.

DOROTHY hands over one of the bunches of keys.

DOROTHY
I'll call Ed Clayton, he's good and reasonably priced. I'll have him send me a survey report and have one for you as well.

FAWN smiles.

FAWN
I really DO appreciate your looking out for me Mrs Felix… I hope you don't think I was being rude.

DOROTHY returns the smile
DOROTHY
No… I think you're doing quite well at what must be a very difficult time, Fawn. With your parents gone too, you're on your own. I think you're a very brave young lady.

FAWN
I'll be in touch after I read the survey and looked the place over.

Both women rise to their feet and shake hands. FAWN leaves and DOROTHY resumes her seat and flicks on her intercom.

DOROTHY
Sarah? Get me the Amityville Mayor on the line.

9. EXT. PLAYHOUSE – FRONT ENTRANCE – DAY.
FAWN and KYLE – complete with rucksacks – approach the theatre, stop and look up at the shabby frontage.

FAWN
Well..?

KYLE

Well what?

FAWN
Well what do you think? It's not much, is it?

KYLE
(GRINNING)It's more than we had before!

FAWN
I still don't know why you want to spend the weekend in a shitty old theatre…

KYLE
Because I get to spend it with you!

FAWN
Kyle, I don't want you getting the wrong idea about this weekend. Nothing's going to happen, okay! NOTHING!
KYLE
(FAUX INNOCENCE) Nothing like that crossed my mind, babe!

FAWN
It'd better not.

They begin walking along the front of the building.

KYLE
(SLIGHTLY BITTER)Besides, with the freakin' Brady Bunch for company I think campfire songs is about as exciting as it's gonna get. (PAUSE) Why'd you have to invite THEM anyway? An airhead and a couple of geeks…

FAWN
Indy's NOT an airhead; she's my best friend. And you shouldn't be bitching about your own brother like that, either. Jevan's been so kind to me since… well, you know.

KYLE
Jevan may be my brother but aside from blood we have NOTHING in common. And he's only being nice to you because he's got a 'thing' for you…

FAWN

He does not! He's genuine. (BEAT) And how can he have a thing for me when you're always saying that you think he's gay!?

KYLE
Well he never goes anywhere without that fag buddy of his.

FAWN
Matt's coming this weekend, too.

KYLE
(SNIGGERS)What did I tell you?

FAWN
You think everyone's gay!
KYLE wiggles his eyebrows slyly.

KYLE
I'm not!

They arrive at the side of the building by the stage door. FAWN takes out the bunch of keys.

KYLE
Did that surveyor dude get back to you?

FAWN
No.

KYLE
You didn't pay him, right?

FAWN
Mrs Felix was taking care of it.

KYLE
She probably just kept the money.

FAWN
Not everyone thinks like you, Kyle. (BEAT)Here.

She hands KYLE the piece of paper with the alarm system code on it.

KYLE

What's this?

FAWN
The code for the alarm system.

She unlocks the door and opens it. Immediately the alarm begins to bleep.

FAWN
Well go ahead! The panel is just down the stairs.

FAWN pushes the reluctant KYLE through the open door. She looks in after him but remains outside.

10. INT. PLAYHOUSE – STAGE DOOR AREA – DAY.
KYLE cautiously makes his way down into the darkened interior.

11. EXT. PLAYHOUSE – STAGE DOOR – DAY.
FAWN tries to see what's happening inside but remains out on the street.

KYLE
(V/O) Where? I can't see a damn thing here!

FAWN
Look on the right. (BEAT) Come ON! It'll go off!

KYLE
(V/O) I think I found it. (BEAT) I can't read the number.

FAWN
Kyle!!

KYLE
Just gimme a sec.

FAWN
What are you DOING?

The beeping ceases. A grinning KYLE peers around the edge of the door.

KYLE
Just call me Blaker the Faker!

FAWN
Asshole!

KYLE
(FAUX HORROR VOICE)Come on in my pretty!

12. INT. PLAYHOUSE – STAGE DOOR AREA – DAY.
It's very quiet. Unconsciously FAWN talks in a whisper.

FAWN
There should be some kinda switch to turn the power on. What does the paper say?

KYLE
It's okay, I've found it.

KYLE flicks the switch and the lights come on. FAWN allows the door to click shut behind her. They stand in silence for a second.

13. INT. PLAYHOUSE – PLANT ROOM – DAY.
Lights come on and pipes begin to vibrate. It's as if the building is waking up.

14. INT. PLAYHOUSE – STAGE DOOR AREA – DAY.

FAWN
Wow… It's so quiet. Kind of creepy…

KYLE
(UNUSUALLY SUBDUED) Yeah…

FAWN
Do you think it's haunted?

KYLE
(RETURNING TO FORM) Nope! Indy hasn't shown up yet!

FAWN
(WITHERINGLY) Fun-ee. Fun-ee!

(SFX. Operatic singing)

FAWN
 Can you hear anything?

They both strain to listen. Nothing.

KYLE
Aw, come on! There's nothing here. It's just a big empty building!

FAWN
Quiet! I thought I heard singing!

KYLE
Hey, maybe the ghosts are going to put on a show for us!

FAWN
I'm serious! Just listen.

Again they both strain to listen. Suddenly there is a terrific banging sound behind them. They both jump. Someone is hammering on the door. FAWN gasps and KYLE swears.
 KYLE
 FUCK!!

KYLE swings the door open. INDY, JEVAN and MATT are outside. JEVAN and MATT are loaded down with sleeping bag, groceries etc. INDY is carrying nothing other than her handbag.

KYLE
What the fuck are you trying to do?

The trio come in through the door which slams shut behind them.

JEVAN
Why don't you turn your fucking cell phone on?

KYLE
My cell phone is on you asswipe!

JEVAN
Well you weren't answering!

KYLE takes out his phone, looks at it and then waves it in Jevan's face.

KYLE
No signal, dude!

JEVAN
We've been wandering around and around the place looking for the door. It's all boarded up out there!

FAWN
(TAKING A MORE CONCILITORY TONE) Sorry, we should have told you. It's all boarded up to keep out intruders. This is only way in.

JEVAN
(SMILES AT FAWN) Yeah, well…

INDY has been looking around herself and not really enjoying the experience much.

INDY
Jeez, Fawn. Is this IT?
FAWN
Well what did you expect?

INDY
I don't know but it looks kinda… boring.

KYLE
This is the stage door entrance. They don't go for a lot of glamour back here.

JEVAN
So where are we gonna be sleeping?

KYLE
I guess we should look for the dressing rooms.

They head off down the stairs.

INDY
Do you think they have cable here..?

15. INT. PLAYHOUSE – DRESSING ROOM #1 – DAY.

The room is small with a dressing bench and a couple of lighted mirrors with chairs in front. There's also a couch in the room but nothing else. The door opens and KYLE pokes his head round it. He looks for the light switch, finds it and flicks it on.

KYLE
Yeah, this is it.

Everyone follows him into the room. JEVAN and MATT dump their loads onto the bench and the couch.

FAWN
It's too small. We can't all sleep in here.

JEVAN
I'll take a look next door.

JEVAN goes out and MATT automatically follows. KYLE nods after them

KYLE
(GRINNING) What did I tell you..?

INDY
(PUZZLED SMILE) Am I missing something?

FAWN
No. Kyle thinks that Jevan and Matt are gay.

INDY
They ARE!?

FAWN
No. He's just being a douche...

KYLE
Why does suspecting someone of being gay make me a douche? We're all equal nowadays.

FAWN
Because, Kyle, you use it as an insult - a term of abuse. You know Jev

and Matt aren't gay but you accuse them because it's a way of getting at them. THAT'S why you're a douche.

The reprimand seems to delight KYLE. JEVAN and MATT return.

JEVAN
There's another room next door about the same size. Why don't you lovely ladies stay here while we go next door?

The boys gather up their share of the bags etcetera and leave the room to go next door. INDY looks around the room like her eyes aren't enjoying the journey very much. She wafts away a fly (SFX)
INDY
Don't tell me there aren't any beds!

FAWN
No, Indy. This isn't a hotel. I told you things would be basic.

INDY
Yeah, but I didn't think we'd be going back to like the Stone Age!

FAWN
Would it help if I let you have the couch?

INDY
(GRINS) You're soooo good to me! (BEAT) So are you gonna be… with Kyle?

INDY inclines her head in the direction that the boys have gone.

FAWN
(MOCK OUTRAGE) No!

INDY
Does Kyle know that?

FAWN
Yes, he does!

INDY
(GIGGLING) Maybe he'll start a rumour about us!?

FAWN

Only if he was part of it.

INDY
Eew! I'm gonna pass...

Both girls laugh. FAWN holds up an air mattress.

FAWN
This is the only thing that's going to get inflated this weekend!

Both girls giggle.

16. INT. PLAYHOUSE – DRESSING ROOM #2 – DAY.

The room is similar in all respects to the first room. The boys enter.
Kyle drops his bags and jumps onto the couch.

KYLE
Called!

JEVAN
You're welcome to it. Probably full of bugs!

KYLE
I'll take my chances. Besides, I don't think I'll be spending too much
time here, if you know what I mean.

JEVAN
(SARCASTIC) No, what DO you mean?

KYLE
Just that I won't be sleeping alone…

JEVAN
(SICKLY VOICE) Aw! Did you bring your little Care Bear with you?
How sweet!

MATT splutters trying to suppress a giggle. KYLE rounds on him.

KYLE
What's so funny, Butthead?

MATT

(VERY QUIET) Nothin'.

KYLE
(TO JEVAN) You don't think I want to spend the night in here with you two, do you? I wouldn't want to be a third wheel.

JEVAN
Shut up, Kyle. Don't you ever quit?

KYLE
Sorry, Beavis!

Before things can develop into an all-out fight, the door opens and the girls come in clutching their air mattresses.

INDY
Can any of you guys help? I can't seem to get this thing up.
It's KYLE's turn to snigger. He points to MATT.

KYLE
How about Butthead over there? He'll blow into it. He can make believe he's kissing Beavis.

MATT colours up but takes the mattress off INDY anyway.

MATT
Do you want me to take a look at it?

INDY
(SICKLY SWEET VOICE) Would you? (BEAT) Come on then.

INDY and MATT leave the room.

KYLE
Well thank God he's gone. I couldn't get a word in.

FAWN
Here, make yourself useful.

FAWN tosses her air mattress over to KYLE. It lands covering his head. He pulls it off and looks at the valve then gets busy inflating the thing.

JEVAN
So what are you doing with the place?

FAWN
I don't know yet.

JEVAN
I knew your dad owned a business but I didn't know he owned a theatre!

FAWN
Hey, you know, neither did I!

JEVAN
So what do you know about the place?

FAWN
Nothing really. Mr Stewart is looking into the history.

JEVAN
Mr. Stewart? From school? No kidding? He teaches geography class though!

FAWN
Just because he's a geography teacher doesn't mean to say he can't take an interest in local history. Coach Baker goes bird watching, doesn't he?

JEVAN
Yeah, true.

FAWN
Mr. Stewart's been good to me since mom and dad died.

KYLE breaks off from inflating the mattress.

KYLE
I think he's a creep. He's got a motive and it's nothing to do with history.

FAWN
No, it's nothing like that. I can tell. And if anyone's gay, he is!

KYLE finishes inflating the bed and puts the bung in.

KYLE
Filled Kyle style! 100% guaranteed.

JEVAN
Yeah, guaranteed to be full of hot air...

KYLE tosses the inflated mattress at JEVAN.

17. INT. DANNEMORA BOOKSTORE – DAY.

VICTOR STEWART enters the bookstore. He browses for a while but obviously can't find what he's looking for. The CLERK is sitting behind the desk and as STEWART passes by, the CLERK looks up.

CLERK
May I help you?

STEWART
Hi. Yes. Erm, I'm looking of the local history section, please.

The CLERK nods over STEWART's shoulder.

CLERK
Directly behind you at the start of the aisle.

STEWART goes to the indicated shelves, sorts through a few titles but quickly realises that there's nothing of any help. He returns to the desk.

STEWART
Look, I sorry. I'm making some notes about Amityville's history. I need some more in-depth information about the town's buildings. I'm just wondering if you'd got anything else.

CLERK
Well I don't think we have anything further along those lines so I would suggest you got to the Amityville Library. Sorry.

STEWART nods a little dejectedly and heads for the door.

18. EXT. PLAYHOUSE – FRONTAGE – DAY.

Establishing shot.

19. INT. PLAYHOUSE – DRESSING ROOM #1 – DAY.

The group has once again assembled and are deciding what they're going to do.

FAWN
Okay. So now what?

KYLE
I dunno…

FAWN
Well this was your idea...

MATT
We could take a look around…

KYLE
(REFERING TO MATT) Listen to the brains of the outfit.

JEVAN
You have a better idea?

KYLE
Well, well… Sounds to me you just want an excuse to pair up with your boyfriend for some 'tender time'…

JEVAN rounds on his brother wide-eyed and snarling.

JEVAN
Cut the shit out, Kyle!

The move is uncharacteristic and startles everyone, KYLE included. KYLE tries to rally but he's genuinely shaken by the fire in JEVAN's eyes.

KYLE
(NERVOUS LAUGH) Stay frosty, brother! Just a little joke!

As fast as it arrived, JEVAN's rage departs. His voice takes on a more reasonable tone but it seems even he was a little unnerved by his outburst.

JEVAN
Do you see anyone laughing? (BEAT) Just leave it alone.
The atmosphere is tense, shot through with a streak of pure awkwardness. INDY attempts to defuse things.

INDY
Hey, why don't we split into groups. 'Scooby Doo'-style?

KYLE rolls his eyes at FAWN who supresses a smirk.

FAWN
(TO KYLE) Okay, Fred, do you want to come with Daphne?

INDY
(GENUINELY ALARMED)Hey, I'm not the geeky one! I don't wanna be the one with the glasses!

MATT
Velma… The one with the glasses. Her name's Velma.

INDY
I'm NOT being Velma!

MATT
I'll come with you…

INDY
Who does that make you?

MATT
Erm… Shaggy I guess…

INDY
(AMUSED, TO JEVAN) Hey, I guess that makes you Scooby! I least I didn't end up as the DOG!

JEVAN is now back to normal and looks as if he couldn't care less.
JEVAN
Whatever.

FAWN
Okay. Let's go explore!

They turn towards the door ready leave and something dark and shapeless wipes the camera.

INDY
What was that?!

KYLE
What was what?

INDY
Someone just ran past the doorway.

KYLE
(DISMISSIVELY) Aw, bullshit!

INDY
I'm not lying Kyle! Something just ran past the door!

KYLE
(SNORTING) SomeTHING..? Not someONE?

INDY
Some… ONE ran past the door!

KYLE
(MOCKINGLY) Well you'd better go find them then, hadn't you?

They all file out of room and head in different directions leaving JEVAN alone. He sits alone totally disinterested in thing.

JEVAN
(UNDER BREATH)Scooby… Fuckin' dog…

JEVAN looks around the room and goes over to the box of groceries. He spots a packet of cookies sticking out of the top and takes it out. He raises his eyebrows appreciatively, opens the packet and helps himself to a couple of the cookies.

JEVAN
Scooby snacks!

He munches on one of them. He's deep in thought. There's the sound of a fly buzzing around his head (SFX). Not paying much attention, he wafts it away. His eye glaze momentarily just as they did early when he threatened KYLE. Suddenly he gets to his feet and leaves the room in the direction FAWN and KYLE took.

20. EXT. VICTOR STEWART'S HOUSE – DAY.

STEWART leaves the house carrying a bag. He gets into his car.

21. INT. PLAYHOUSE – STAIRWELL LEADING TO THE CIRCLE – DAY.

INDY and MATT are climbing the stairs. MATT is carrying a torch to light their way.

INDY
Kyle's such a jerk sometimes.

MATT
Yeah. What did you see?

INDY
Just something run past the door. I couldn't make out what it was though.

MATT
Maybe it was just shadows. This place is too dark.

INDY
This wasn't any kind of shadow. Do YOU think I'm lying, too?

MATT
No! No... Just thinking through the possibilities is all... Maybe a dog got in..?

INDY
A six-foot high dog? (SARCASTIC) Yeah, right!

MATT
Sorry... I don't know.(BEAT) You're right, Kyle is a jerk though...

INDY
Why d'you let him give you such a hard time? Why don't you stand up

for yourself?

MATT
I don't know...

INDY
(MIMICKING)"I don't know, I don't know, I don't know" Do you
know ANYTHING?
MATT
I don't...

They arrive at in the circle lobby. It's obviously deserted and dark.
MATT shines the torch around. He points it at the doors leading through
to the balcony.

MATT
I guess they must lead onto the circle.

INDY
Why is the balcony called the circle?

MATT
(WITHOUT THINKING) I don't know...

22. INT. PLAYHOUSE – SCENERY WORKSHOP – DAY.

KYLE and FAWN are looking around. There's nothing much to see
and KYLE is already cooling on the whole idea of spending the weekend in
a such a 'dump'.

FAWN
This must be where they made all the scenery and stuff.

KYLE
(DISINTERESTEDLY) Right...

FAWN
Do you think there is anyone else in here? You know, like Indy said?

KYLE
She's dumber that a bag of hammers. I wouldn't trust her to tell me that
she was wet if she was taking a swim.

FAWN
She isn't dumb!

KYLE
No? Remember when she asked how come the head of Al-Qaeda got to be President?

FAWN
She just gets confused sometimes…

KYLE
Yeah, like seeing things that aren't there.

FAWN
Maybe there is someone else in here.

KYLE
Nah, she's just taking the 'Scooby-Doo' stuff too seriously. (BEAT)Hey, perhaps it's the janitor?

FAWN
(LAUGHING) And he would have got away with it if it wasn't for us meddling kids!

23. INT. PLAYHOUSE – FRONT OF HOUSE – DAY.

JEVAN wanders into the foyer with his torch. He tries the main doors but they are boarded-up and don't move an inch. He shines his torch into the box office but there's nothing much interesting to see. He looks into the manager's office and sees a sleeping bag and other bits of camping equipment. He turns to leave and comes face-to-face with a girl standing directly behind him. He jumps backwards in surprise at the encounter.

JEVAN
Fuck! You scared the shit out of me!

WENDY
Who the fuck are you? What are you doing in my place?

JEVAN looks the newcomer up and down.

JEVAN
Your place!? My friend owns this. It's hers. You're trespassing!

JEVAN gets a proper look at her. She's pretty but hard-looking. She's obviously a Goth/Rocker type – all her clothes are black: jeans, boots, jacket and gloves. She's wearing a lot of silver jewellery – skulls etc. - and has heavy make-up.

WENDY
You're lying! Nobody owns this place. It's mine. I found it!

JEVAN
Of course somebody owns it! Fawn Harriman owns it. She's here's somewhere. She can prove it.

WENDY
Well I'm not leaving!

JEVAN
Well, I don't know about that... What's your name?

WENDY
Mary-Jane. What the fuck's it got to do with you?

JEVAN
Nothing. Just making conversation. My name's Jev... Jevan.

WENDY
Mors Adorate...

JEVAN
That's Latin! It means 'Adore Death'.

WENDY is impressed and her front drops a little.

WENDY
Check out the big brain on Jev! Where'd you learn Latin, Poindexter?

JEVAN
Bits here and there.

WENDY extends a gloved fist.

WENDY
Wendy…

JEVAN dutifully bumps the fist. WENDY offers JEVAN a can of beer.

WENDY
Want a cold one? Well, a warm one now…

JEVAN shakes his head. She fishes in her jacket pocket and pulls out a packet of cigarettes and a lighter.

WENDY
Smoke?

JEVAN shakes again. Wendy raises an eyebrow.

WENDY
Well aren't you just too much fun?

WENDY opens her beer, takes a pull then open the cigarette packet, removes a cigarette and lights it.

WENDY
How did you get the lights to work?

JEVAN
With the switch…

WENDY
When I tried them they didn't work.

JEVAN
Fawn must have turned on the power she got here (BEAT) How did you get in here? There's an alarm.

WENDY
Is there? I found a grating around back. I lifted it up and dropped into the basement. I didn't hear no alarms.

JEVAN
Why?

WENDY
Maybe the basement isn't wired up.

JEVAN
No, I mean why did you want to come in here?

WENDY
I needed a place to go.

JEVAN
Don't you have a home?

WENDY
Not really… My dad's a bum. He never had much time for me and since his girlfriend moved in it's been even worse.

JEVAN
Mom?

WENDY
What about her? I wouldn't know her if I passed her in the street. She walked out when I was six.

JEVAN
But why come here?

WENDY
(SHRUGS) Why not? It's empty and dry. Well it WAS empty. Anyway, I like it, it's got a vibe.

JEVAN
You can't stay. Well, at least not without talking to Fawn.

WENDY
(DEFINETLY)I'm not leaving!
JEVAN
Maybe you won't have to. Let's go find Fawn.

24. EXT. HIGHWAY – LEVEL-CROSSING – DAY.
VICTOR STEWART's car draws up to a level-crossing. A freight train is passing by.

25. INT. VICTOR STEWART'S CAR – DAY.

The passing wagons have a hypnotic effect on STEWART and his mind goes back to his last hours back in the UK just prior to his leaving for the US. The passing wagons segue into…

26. EXT. UK - 'THE CROSS KEYS' PUB – DAY.

FLASHBACK …a red London bus passing in front of the pub.

27. INT. UK - 'THE CROSS KEYS' PUB – DAY.

STEWART enters the pub. Behind the bar is the landlady, KAREN. She spots him and smiles. She's got a soft spot for him.

KAREN
Hello Vic. Come in for your last pint of decent beer before the off?

STEWART
Something like that.

KAREN takes a glass and starts to pour the beer.

KAREN
So when are you leaving?

She passes the beer over to him and he hands her the right change.

STEWART
I actually leave the village tomorrow morning.

KAREN
You won't get beer like that in America, you know.

STEWART takes a pull at the beer and pulls a fake grimace.

STEWART
No, it'll have taste…

Some of the beer slops down his shirt front.

KAREN

Serves you right! You'll miss me, you know you will. (BEAT) By the way, your girlfriend is in.

KAREN nods towards an older lady who is sitting at a table along with the local vicar and his wife. KAREN bats her eyelashes in an exaggerated manner and simpers at STEWART.

STEWART
Behave yourself! Celia's a respected scientist!

KAREN
(THOUGHTFULLY) Don't you think that's a bit weird though?

STEWART
What? Being a scientist?

KAREN
Her living with her nephew and his wife.

STEWART
What's weird about that?
KAREN
Hasn't it every occurred to you. She's a palaeontologist and he's the local Vicar... (BEAT THEN PROMPTS) 'and never the twain shall meet..?'

STEWART
Karen, I have absolutely no idea what you're talking about.

KAREN
(ROLLS EYES) She spends Mondays to Fridays telling her students that life took billions of years to evolve and he spends his Sundays telling his congregation it took seven days! What do you think that means?

STEWART
They have nothing to argue about on Saturdays..?

KAREN
Just seems funny to me that they can coexist...

STEWART

I don't see why. She's a member of the congregation and he goes out on the odd dig or two with her.

KAREN
Don't you think that science and religion are sort of opposites?

STEWART takes a pull at his beer and his bottom lip comes out as he mulls the concept over.

STEWART
I suppose. They seem happy enough though. There must be some common ground between science and religion. Tell you what, I'll ask!

KAREN
Don't you dare!

28. EXT. HIGHWAY – LEVEL-CROSSING – DAY.
We return to the present. The freight train clears the crossing and STEWART's car clears the crossing.

29. INT. PLAYHOUSE – HOUSE CIRCLE – DAY.
INDY and MATT have made their way to the top of the theatre and are on the balcony overlooking the stalls and the stage. MATT is leaning way over the rail.

INDY
What are you doing?

MATT
I don't know.

INDY
You don't know? Thinking of jumping?

MATT
I wonder how far out I can lean?

INDY
Do you think anyone ever fell from here? You know like in the OLD days? Do you think anyone ever JUMPED?

MATT
Why would anyone want to jump?

INDY
You know, if they were like depressed or had been in a fight with their girlfriend or something.

MATT
Maybe… But why would anyone want to buy a ticket just to haul their ass up here and then jump off? You could shoot yourself and save 5 bucks.

INDY
What if they like got depressed during the show and THEN jumped?

MATT
Well, I suppose it depends on just how shitty the show was.

INDY
Aw, come on, let's go. This is boring and I'm getting hungry.
They make their way back to the doors. As they leave there is a drawn-out scream from back on the balcony (SFX). They exchange shocked glances and rush back to the rail. They look over. Lying far below on the gangway is FAWN. A rapidly expanding pool of blood around her head. INDY screams. They turn and run for the stairs.

30. INT. PLAYHOUSE – AUDITORIUM – DAY.
INDY and MATT burst into the auditorium and cross to the spot beneath the balcony and look up. FAWN leans over, looks down, laughs and then vanishes from view. Both are frightened and bewildered.

MATT
What the fuck is going on?!

INDY
(SOBBING) What happened? What HAPPENED?

MATT
We saw her! We saw her right THERE!! (POINTS)There was blood!

INDY
(SOBBING) But she was just up there! (POINTS)
MATT
She must have been fucking around!

INDY
(SLIGHTLY CALMER)Why? That's not funny!

MATT examines the floor then looks up again to check he's in the right spot.

MATT
Where's the blood? It was all over! How..?

MATT spins around looking for a clue as to what's going on.

MATT
How did she get up there so fast? She didn't pass us… and there's only one set of stairs!
There's a noise of doors opening and FAWN and KYLE come in. INDY lunges at FAWN, hammering her with her fists and crying.

INDY
(HYSTERICAL) You stupid bitch!

KYLE pulls INDY away and she subsides into a seat. She sobs brokenly. FAWN and KYLE are astonished.

KYLE
What the hell is going on, Butthead?

MATT points an accusing finger at FAWN.

MATT
I don't know how you did it but that wasn't funny, man! No fucking joke!

KYLE looks from FAWN to MATT and back again. FAWN just looks confused.

FAWN
What are you talking about?! (INDICATING INDY) What's the matter with her?

MATT
(GETTING IN FAWN'S FACE) That stunt was just stone cold! Not funny!

KYLE steps in and pushes MATT in the chest.

KYLE
Just cool your fucking boots, man! Tell me what happened!

MATT cools slightly. INDY is still in shock.

MATT
You must know. You must have helped.

KYLE
I'm going count to five…

MATT
(STILL BREATHING HARD) You KNOW! That balcony stunt! We thought Fawn was dead, man! Actually dead!

FAWN
Dead!? (BEAT) What stunt?

MATT
Making out you'd fallen off the balcony. Then when we ran down here you were up there (POINTS) laughing your ass off!

KYLE
Fuck you! We haven't been near the balcony! We were in back.

KYLE waves a hand in the direction of the stage.

FAWN
We were Matt… We only just got here.

FAWN's tone and obvious sincerity make MATT stop and think for a second. It occurs to him that she couldn't have got down from the balcony in the few seconds after he saw her up there and her and KYLE showing up in the auditorium.

MATT
But… We SAW you. We heard you scream. We looked down and you were lying here (POINTS).

INDY
(SOBBING) It's true, Fawn! We BOTH saw it!

31. INT. PLAYHOUSE – DRESSING ROOM #1 – DAY.

Everyone is back, gathered in the dressing room. The others have been telling JEVAN what's happened. WENDY is also there although in the excitement, no introductions have been made. JEVAN reacts to the account of what's happened with a mix of incredulity and surprise.

JEVAN
Really!? That's weird.

WENDY
Weird stuff happens here all the time.

Everyone's attention turns to WENDY who is sitting on a table.

KYLE
And just who the fuck are you?

JEVAN
Uh… That's Wendy. Wendy, this is, Matt, Indy, Fawn and Kyle. Wendy lives here.

KYLE
What do you mean she 'lives' here?

WENDY
Yeah, I live here.

FAWN
I own this place. You can't come in here without my permission.

WENDY
I have no place else to go. I didn't know you owned it or anyone owned it.

JEVAN
(PLACATINGLY) Look guys, can't Wendy just stay here for the weekend? Come on, it'll be fun.

FAWN
(HESITANTLY) Well, I guess so…

WENDY
Hey, you don't have to do ME no favours! I do just fine on my own!

JEVAN
Woah, woah, woah! Listen, Wendy, why don't you go upstairs to the office and get your stuff. We'll order a pizza! My treat! Come on!

WENDY nods and, eyeing the others up, heads out of the door.
KYLE
Where in hell did you find THAT?

JEVAN
She was camping out in the office out front.

MATT
She looks kinda… cute.

KYLE
(SNORTING) A girl like that would suck you in a blow you out as bubbles!

FAWN
What's with all the make-up and clothes though?

KYLE
Halloween was weeks ago.

JEVAN
Don't start on her, Kyle!

KYLE
Just telling it as I see it… (LOOKING AT MATT) Freakiness loves company, eh?
Again JEVAN's eye's flash with anger.

JEVAN
Quit it, Kyle!

Again Kyle is put on the back-foot by his brother's uncharacteristic outburst.

KYLE
At least we've solved the mystery of the weird shit that's been

happening around here.

FAWN
What do you mean?

KYLE
(INDICATES THE HALLWAY) Aw, Lily Munster's the one who's been pranking us.

JEVAN
No she hasn't. She didn't even know we were here.

KYLE
Sure. And you believe that? We've been stomping around here like a bunch of Transformers! We could've woken the dead!

INDY
That's not funny, Kyle!

FAWN
Well, we can ask her when she comes back.

MATT
That wasn't her we saw from the balcony.

KYLE
Where's she from, anyway?

JEVAN
Local girl I guess. She said something about her mom walking out when she was a kid. Her dad not paying any attention to her and being a douche, so she left.
KYLE
A runaway? Hey, imagine seeing that face on a milk carton! Turn it into cheese!

FAWN
Look, let's just try to forget it. (BEAT) Okay, who's hungry?

Everyone stands around nodding and making affirmative noises.

FAWN
Okay! Let's order pizza!

KYLE
And see if they do a Bat's Eye pie with extra cobwebs for our new friend.

FAWN
There's a menu someplace.

FAWN starts to look for the menu. KYLE takes out his cell phone.

KYLE
My phone's still not working.

Everyone takes out their phones and tries for a signal but it's pretty obvious none of them has a signal.

MATT
Me neither.

JEVAN
Zilch!

INDY
I've got a signal but nothing's going through.

KYLE
Let's try outside.

32. INT. PLAYHOUSE – STAGE DOOR AREA – DAY.
Everyone bar WENDY is gathered at the stage door. KYLE goes to open it but it's locked.

KYLE
(TO FAWN) Did you lock this after we came in?

FAWN
No, I didn't. The other three came in after us. I haven't been here since.

KYLE
Well give me the key.

FAWN hands KYLE the key. KYLE inserts the key into the lock but it doesn't seem to fit. He hands it back to FAWN.

KYLE
That's the wrong damned key!

FAWN
No it isn't. That's the key Mrs Felix gave me. I don't have any others! Try it again.
FAWN hands the key back to KYLE who tries it again. It still doesn't fit.

JEVAN
Try turning it the other way.

KYLE
I can't turn it the other way, dickwad? It doesn't even fit into the lock!

JEVAN
Well it has to! We got in didn't we?

KYLE
Well you try it then, Einstein!

KYLE thrusts the key under JEVAN'S nose. JEVAN takes it and approaches the door. The key still refuse to fit. JEVAN seems to becomes obsessed. He stabs the key uselessly at the lock, his movements becoming more and more frantic and frenzied. He begins to rant in a voice not his own. It's deep and accented.

JEVAN
They've have sealed us in! They've left us! They've left us to die!

JEVAN'S hands are now cut and bleeding but he continues trying to insert the key into the lock.

JEVAN (CONT'D)
We're dying! Sealed in! WE'RE DYING!

The others look bewildered and terrified. INDY begins sobbing again.

KYLE and MATT drag JEVAN back and his frenzy suddenly stops and he slumps but doesn't fall.

KYLE
What the fuck are you doing, man?!

JEVAN seems dazed but recognition is back in his eyes.

MATT
Dude, look at your hands! Are you okay?

JEVAN looks at his bloodied hands.

FAWN
We'd better get him back to the dressing room and take a look at his hands.

INDY
But what about the door? We're locked in!!

KYLE
I still think that freak's got something to do with what's happening here.

33. INT. PLAYHOUSE – DRESSING ROOM #1 – DAY.
The group enter the dressing room. WENDY has set up her bed and is sitting on it smoking a cigarette. KYLE is straight into the attack.

KYLE
Have you been fucking around with the stage door?

WENDY doesn't get up but turns her head to look at him. She seems quite relaxed and unconcerned.

WENDY
I haven't been near the stage door. I got back here and the room was empty. I set up my cot and waited.

KYLE
Look at his hands! (HE INDICATE JEVAN'S HANDS) He cut himself up trying to make the key to work.

WENDY sits up and she looks genuinely concerned.

WENDY
(TO JEVAN) Are you okay?

JEVAN still looks a little punchy but nods.

JEVAN
Yeah… I must've caught my hand on something sharp.

FAWN
I don't have any Band Aids but we can at least try to clean this up for you.

They file out shooting backward glances at WENDY.

34. INT. PLAYHOUSE – WASHROOM – DAY.
FAWN is bathing JEVAN's hand in one of the wash basins.

FAWN
I can't see any cuts. Where does it hurt?

JEVAN frowns and examines his hands a little closer.

JEVAN
Actually, it doesn't. (BEAT) Let me just wash my hands.

JEVAN washes his hands under the running water.

JEVAN
No marks, no blood, no cuts. Nothing! Not a trace!
35. INT. PLAYHOUSE – DRESSING ROOM #1 – DAY.
FAWN and JEVAN re-enter the room. FAWN grab JEVAN's arm thrusts it forward so everyone can see his hand.

FAWN
Look!

KYLE
Oh come on! This is beyond strange now! We all saw his hands all cut up to shit!

INDY
I don't like any of this, we should leave! I want to go home!

KYLE
How? We can't open the door?

FAWN
A building this size there must be more than one way out.

KYLE
The street doors are boarded up!
FAWN
What about windows?

KYLE
It's a theatre! Theatres don't have windows!

FAWN
But there must be SOME windows.

JEVAN
Hey, wait. (TO WENDY) Didn't you say you came in by a grate in the basement?

WENDY
Yeah.

KYLE
Show us where.

36. INT. PLAYHOUSE – BASEMENT – DAY.

A door opens and light floods in illuminating a flight of stairs leading down into the basement. The party enters with WENDY at the front. They cautiously make their way down into the darkness. WENDY leads them over to the far wall and uses her torch to highlight the grating.

WENDY
This is it.

KYLE finds something to stand on and gives the grille a heave. It gives a fraction but doesn't open. Grey daylight can be seen but the grille only opens a tiny fraction.

INDY
(PANICKY) Push it!

KYLE
I am pushing it, airhead! I think something's blocking it. Jevan, lend a hand!

JEVAN just stands staring like he's in some kind of trance.

KYLE (CONT'D)
Come on!

JEVAN is still unresponsive. KYLE turns his attention to MATT.

KYLE (CONT'D)
You. Help!

MATT clumsily climbs up next to KYLE and they both push. They strain but the grille doesn't move.

KYLE (CONT'D)
It's not going to give.

KYLE and MATT climb down. KYLE turns to JEVAN.

KYLE (CONT'D)
What the hell's wrong with you?

JEVAN has that strange look about him again.

JEVAN
Buried… Buried… No light… No air…

KYLE disguises his unease in threatening behaviour.

KYLE
Just cut that bullshit out will you? Stupid voices and shit. You're freaking people out.

JEVAN seems to recover himself and INDY begins to sob again.

INDY
This is a nightmare! We're trapped!

FAWN
Look, there must be an explanation for all of this. (TO KYLE) What do you think's happening?

KYLE
I still say someone's in here trying to pranks us and freak us out!

INDY
But what about the keys and the blood on Jevan's hands? And us seeing Fawn dead?

KYLE
Someone's changed the locks. Easy enough to do. Maybe there was something in the keyhole to squirt blood.

MATT
But what about seeing Fawn dead?

KYLE
It's a theatre, Butthead! There must be all kinds of stage equipment, projectors and shit laying around here.

INDY
Let's just go!
FAWN
You really think someone else is in here? Pranking us?

KYLE
Well SHE got in. And I still think she's got something to do with all this shit. Probably buddies of hers having a good laugh.

FAWN
But what about Jevan acting all weird?

KYLE
That's easily explained… He's an asshole…

INDY
Do you think Kyle is right? Is it someone trying to scare us?

MATT

I don't know.

MATT
Yeah, maybe he's right. I mean, all of that stuff could have been done with projectors just like he said. I mean ghosts and shit don't really exist, do they?

INDY
(QUIETLY TO MATT) Maybe they do… (LOUDER TO WENDY) Hey, do you want to take that habit outta here? That's like so disrespectful of you.

INDY
She's just SO creepy!

JEVAN
She's just a little different is all.

KYLE
Do you think it's weird that the strange shit started happening as soon as she showed up?

JEVAN
Weird shit's been happening the entire time we've been here.

FAWN
Just how long has she been here?

JEVAN
I don't know. I never asked.

KYLE
Well, I guess we'll just have a little talk with Morticia Addams when she gets back.

INDY
Aren't we forgetting something? How do we get out of here?

KYLE
We'll have to find some way of breaking the door down.
FAWN
But I want to know if there's anyone else in here? This is MY property

and I'm not going to be scared out of it by a bunch of douche bags!

KYLE
Okay, let's take another look around. Let's look into every nook and cranny.

KYLE
Tell us what kind of 'stuff' you've heard!

WENDY
Just the building settling, you know… And… Well, music…

FAWN
Music..? What music?

WENDY
I don't know what it is. Old stuff my grandma used to listen to. I just figured it was coming from outside but there's nothing much around this neighbourhood…

WENDY
You know, your friend is a major asshole. Is he always so suspicious of people?

JEVAN
Actually, he's my brother…

WENDY
I'm sorry.

JEVAN
That's fine, he IS an asshole.

WENDY
No, I'm sorry you have to have him for a brother. He thinks highly of himself, doesn't he?

JEVAN
He always has.

WENDY

Is Fawn his girlfriend?

JEVAN
Yeah, but I don't know why she puts up with him.

WENDY
Why does she owns this place anyway?

JEVAN
Her folks died in a fire a while back.

WENDY
Wow, that's tough.

JEVAN
Yeah, she's all alone now.

WENDY
Kind of know how she feels...

INDY
Eww! This is gross! Everything is so grimy and dirty! Let's go! Nobody's been in here for like a million years!

MATT
Yeah, there's nothing here.

INDY
I still think that creepy girl is behind all of this. She's just so weird!

MATT
Aw, she's alright.

INDY
Do you think she's hot..?

MATT
(AWKWARD) Nah... She's... Well... She's... You know...

INDY
Should I be jealous?

MATT
Jealous..? Erm… Well…

INDY
Oh my God!! Oh my God!! Oh my God!! Did you see that? It was like the size of a dog!

MATT
Just a rat. To be expected in a place like this. Nothing to be scared of.

INDY
You ran like a freaking gold medallist!

MATT
Erm… I was just making sure you were alright and that it couldn't get out.

INDY
No WAY am I going back in there!

MATT
We don't have to. There's no-one hiding there. Let's go look someplace else.

FAWN
Do you think anyone's up there?

KYLE
If there is, they can stay there. I'm not climbing up to take a look.

KYLE
Babe, you okay? I heard you scream.

FAWN
It was horrible! The stage and everywhere was filled with people all pointing at me and screaming!!

KYLE

Tough crowd, eh?

FAWN
I'm serious, Kyle, it was a nightmare! I thought they were going to kill me.

KYLE
Babe, you okay? I heard you scream.

FAWN
It was horrible! The stage and everywhere was filled with people all pointing at me and screaming!!

KYLE
Tough crowd, eh?

FAWN
I'm serious, Kyle, it was a nightmare! I thought they were going to kill me.

KYLE
Hey, that's all it was. It was just a nightmare. I was there the whole time and I would've been able to see or hear if there'd been anyone else.

FAWN
It seemed so real though.

KYLE
Okay, let's head back to the room. I'm sure the other are done by now.

STEWART
I'd like a room please.

CLERK
You don't want to stay in Amityville.

STEWART
I DO want to stay in Amityville!

CLERK
No vacancies! No vacancies!

STEWART
Yeah, but there ARE vacancies! I saw the 'vacancy' sign!

CLERK
No. No vacancies now!

STEWART
But there are no cars out there! You've got plenty of rooms.

CLERK
But we don't have any room for YOU!

STEWART
I don't understand… Look, I've got money.

STEWART (CONT'D)
I've got money. How much do you want?

CLERK
Oh, thank you very much!

CLERK (CONT'D)
I've got a room for you!
INDY
Hey, are you okay? You look sick.

FAWN
Yeah. I'm good. Just got a little dizzy back there.

KYLE
She fainted but she's okay now.

JEVAN
Did you guys find anything?

KYLE
Nothing.

JEVAN
Us neither.

INDY
(HOPEFULLY) Do you think they might have gone?

WENDY
I don't think there was ever anyone here.

KYLE
We should make some food. (TO FAWN) Maybe that's why you passed out.

FAWN
Yeah, I guess.

FAWN
You're welcome to join us…

WENDY
No, it's okay. I've got my own stuff.

INDY
Why are we sitting here talking about food? We should be trying to get out!

KYLE
We've tried. Remember!

INDY
(GETTING HYSTERICAL) So we're going to stay in here the rest of our lives!?

KYLE

Don't be so dumb! We need to think about it. It's not like we're going to run out of air or anything, is it? We can think about it while we're eating. I'm hungry even if you're not.

FAWN
(TO INDY) Look, no one's been hurt, have they? Some strange things have happened but nothing really dangerous.

INDY
Not yet!

FAWN
Kyle thinks someone is trying to scare us for some reason. Well, if they are, we're ready for them now.

KYLE
So can I cook or can I cook?

JEVAN
Yeah, 'cos it takes a lot of talent to open-up a couple of cans of spicy beans…

KYLE
Hey, I didn't see you falling over your feet to help out, little brother!

JEVAN
Yeah, but at least I don't pull all that 'new man' shit just because I can use a can opener.

FAWN
Okay you two, let's not start another fight.

INDY
Kyle! That's so gross!

KYLE
What is this, Judgement day? (BEAT) I'm going next door.

FAWN
Come on, Jev. Let's try and keep the peace.

JEVAN
(SIGHS) I guess…

MATT
I'll just... You know...
WENDY
(SARDONICALLY) Anyone else? (BEAT)You guys are just one big pot of love stew, huh?

FAWN
I think Matt just felt a little outnumbered.
WENDY
What about the other two?

FAWN
They just rub each other up the wrong way. Some brothers are like that. (BEAT) You got any brothers or sisters?

WENDY
I have a sister younger than me. Mom took her when she went. I haven't see her since. You got any?

FAWN
No.

WENDY
What about your parents? Jev said there was a fire or something...

INDY
You're a little nosy, aren't you?

FAWN
It's okay, Indy. Maybe I should talk about it more. I've got pretty tired of people tip-toeing around me since it happened.

WENDY
What happened?

FAWN
My folks owned a house up in Canada. We used to go up there every summer. I used to hate it when I was younger because it meant spending summer away from my friends...

JEAN

Fawn, why do we have to go through this every year?

FAWN
Because every year I get dragged up to that dumb house where there's
nothing to do and no-one to talk to!

JEAN
Go to the lake then.

FAWN
That's no fun on your own!

JEAN
Well, read a book! Your dad has tons of books up there!

FAWN
They're all history books! Why would I want to study when I'm on
vacation?

JEAN
So buy yourself a magazine then! But you're not going to be sitting
around all summer watching TV like you do every year!

FAWN
And why can't we have cable up there?

JEAN
Frank, can you please talk to your daughter? She's being impossible!

FRANK
We go there to get AWAY from things like that.

FAWN
But daddy, it's boring! I don't know why I have to go with you.

FRANK
We don't like to think of you just rattling around at home all on your
own.

JEAN
Besides, it's tradition! We've been going every year since you were

born…

FAWN
Well don't you think it's time that we broke with tradition. I'm old enough to make my own decisions now.

WENDY
Wow… Heavy.

FAWN
I get this crazy feeling that if I'd kind of carried on with the 'tradition' they would have been okay. There wouldn't have been a fire.

INDY
That IS crazy! If you'd gone with them you would have been in the fire, too.

FAWN
They were found in bed, just lying there. If I was there I might have been able to help…

WENDY
Help? How?

FAWN
I might have woken up and been able to warn them…

WENDY
No, I think your friend is right. It would have been you as well if you were there.

FAWN
What've you got there?

INDY
What is it?

KYLE
It's a Ouiji board!

WENDY
'Ouija'. It originates from the French and German language meaning 'yes.'

FAWN
Where in the hell did you get that?

MATT
Erm… I bought it. It was my grandmother's.

FAWN
Well what did you bring it here for?!

MATT
Well… I guess I thought it might be… you know… fun.

INDY
Those things can be dangerous! I've seen things about them.

KYLE
Yeah, in movies. This is real life, remember?

INDY
I don't want to fool around with that thing!

WENDY
I think it's cool!

INDY
Well you would!

FAWN
(TO MATT) I don't know… After the kind of day we've had, what makes you think we'd want to play with that thing?

MATT
I packed it last night. I didn't know weird stuff was going to happen when we got here… I wasn't going to say anything.

INDY
So why did you?

MATT
I told Jevan and…

FAWN
…He told Kyle?

MATT
Yeah.

KYLE
Aw, come on! Nothin's going to happen! It's just for fun!

FAWN
I don't know. With all that's happened here…

INDY
You can count me out!

KYLE
Done! (TO MATT)Now, how do you make it work?

MATT
Err… Well I've never actually used it before.

WENDY
I know how to do it. For starters, this room is too small. You need to
move to a bigger space for the spirits to resonate.
KYLE
(TO WENDY) You've done this before?

WENDY
Yeah, lots of times…

KYLE
Okay! Let's go!

STEWART
Good evening everyone!

DOCTOR NIGHTINGALE
Hello Victor, darling!

RANDALL
Hi!
LIZ
Hello!

STEWART
May I..?

RANDALL
So you're off tomorrow to pass on some good old Blighty know-now to our colonial cousins

STEWART
Yes. I leave the village tomorrow morning and fly out tomorrow lunchtime.

LIZ
Remind me again where you're going, again, Victor.

STEWART
Upstate New York. A little village called Dannemorra.

LIZ
We used to live in the States. Just ofr a few years. Yes, when Simon was first ordained. But that was on the West Coast. It was Selah in Washington state.

RANDALL
Lovely place though. Very cold winters. Didn't agree with Liz's chilblains!

LIZ
Simon!

DOCTOR NIGHTINGALE
Well Victor, the very best of luck to you! Cheers!

STEWART
(HUMBLY) Thank you!

DOCTOR NIGHTINGALE
Oh, I've got you a little present.

STEWART
"Paleantology: The First Steps And What Lies Beneath Them". Your book!

DOCTOR NIGHTINGALE
I've signed it…

STEWART
"To Victor – Thank you for your friendship and faith." Thank you!

DOCTOR NIGHTINGALE
I hope it'll inspire you to go out and get your hands dirty once in a while!

INDY
Why do we need so many candles?

WENDY
The light from the candles helps the spirits find their way.

KYLE
Now what do we do?

WENDY
Everybody has to place an index finger on the beaker.

KYLE
And..?

WENDY
We move it in a figure eight whilst asking a question.

KYLE
I'll go first... Okay. "Will Jevan meet the boy of his dreams this year or the year after?"

JEVAN
How about, "Will Kyle ever be able to sleep without the light on?"

FAWN
For crying out loud, give it a rest you two! Ask something sensible! What do we do, Wendy?

WENDY
Ask if anyone is there...

KYLE
"Is anyone there..?"

WENDY
Try again.

KYLE
"Is anyone there..?"

.

KYLE
Somebody's pushing it!

FAWN
No one better push! I want to see if this works! Ask another question. Wendy.

WENDY
"Are there spirits in this building?"

MATT
That's weird.

WENDY
"What do the spirits want?"

FAWN
S-I-S-T-E-R. Sister..?

INDY
I told you not to mess with these things! I told you!

KYLE
I still think someone was pushing it. It's all bullshit.

FAWN
I feel like it's connected to me somehow.(BEAT) You know what, I'm
tired. I think I want to go to bed right now.
KYLE
It's still pretty early. I've bought some beers. We can't go to sleep yet.

FAWN
Kyle, I'm real tired… I just want to go to bed. We can make a search for
a way out in the morning. I'm too tired to do anything right now.

KYLE looks around the group to rally support but everyone is nodding
in agreement with FAWN. He decides to change tack. He adopts a
ridiculous smile and goes over to FAWN.

KYLE
So are we going to like lose the Brady Bunch for half an hour..?

FAWN's expression shows that she can't even be bothered to be
contemptuous of KYLE's 'request'.

FAWN
Kyle, just go to bed, huh? …Your OWN bed.

MATT
What are you doing, dude?

JEVAN

I'm going to take a piss.

MATT
What time is it?

JEVAN
It's just after three.

MATT
Can't you wait until morning?

JEVAN
No, my bladder's like a fuckin' basketball, dude!

MATT
Well, try and be more quiet when you come back, huh?

JEVAN
Huh! Yeah! Fuck you too!

INDY
Yeah… I slept okay. I feel better now it's day. I still think Jevan was a douche for screwing with us.

INDY
She didn't even
change before she got into bed! How gross is THAT?
FAWN
(WHISPERING) She got up in the night, too.

INDY
(WHISPERING) I didn't hear that.

FAWN
I'd be surprised if you'd heard anything over all that snoring you were doing!

INDY
(MOCK OUTRAGE) You bitch!

INDY
(EMBARRASSED) I am so sorry! I was aiming at Fawn! Sorry!

WENDY
(DEADPAN) S'okay.

FAWN
Yeah?

MATT
(V/O) Erm… Can I come in?

FAWN
Yeah, it's safe.

MATT
Erm… Have you guys seen Jev this morning?

INDY
No, he hasn't been in here.

FAWN
Maybe he went to the washroom.

MATT
He went in the night but I didn't see him come back.

FAWN
You got up in the night didn't you, Wendy? Did you see him?

WENDY
I went out for a cigarette. I didn't see anything.

INDY
You should knock before entering a lady's bedroom!

KYLE
Show me a lady and I'll do some knocking… Besides, he's

(INDICATES MATT) in here.

FAWN
You didn't know he was in here and Matt knocked before he came in.

INDY
I could've been naked!

KYLE
Which would have put me right off breakfast... (BEAT) Where's my little brother this morning?

FAWN
You haven't seen him either?

KYLE
What do you mean, 'either'?

MATT
He went to the bathroom around 3am. I didn't see him come back.

KYLE
Well he must be around here somewhere!

INDY
Maybe he found a way out?

KYLE
Why would he be looking for a way out on his own at 3am? And he would've come back and told us.

FAWN
(TO WENDY) You said you went out into the hallway for a cigarette. Are you sure you didn't see anything?

WENDY
I told you – nothing.

KYLE
What time was that? Did you go anywhere else?

WENDY
I don't remember the time and when I was through I came back to bed.

KYLE
I'll bet he's just trying to jerk our chains again!

FAWN
So what now?

KYLE
I'm going to go find him!

FAWN
And then what?

KYLE
Well… Get his ass back here for a start! I'm tired of his 'spooky' bullshit games.

FAWN
We'll all go.

INDY
I'm not going! I'm going to wait here… and see if he comes back.

STEWART
Are you okay?

LADY
(DEFENSIVELY) It's just my first-born!

LIBRARIAN
Can I help you, sir?

STEWART
I'm looking for a local history section please…

LIBRARIAN
Why would you want to know our local history?

LIBRARIAN

Ah, yeah! Just around the corner and off to the left!

INDY
Jevan? Jevan is ,that you..? Stop screwing around! This isn't funny, you know! I'm not scared!(BEAT) They've gone looking for you. Kyle said you have to wait here.

FAWN
Where's Indy? Where IS she?

WENDY
I don't know. She wasn't here.

MATT
That scream…

FAWN
I never heard anyone scream like that before!

KYLE
Okay, guys… Let's calm down for a second. Something must have scared her. She must have just run off.

MATT
But that scream…

KYLE
Just shut the fuck up a second! Let me think!(BEAT) Okay, we're looking for them both now. Let's go

KYLE
We'll meet back here.

MATT
(TO WENDY) What do you think happened?

WENDY
I don't know.

MATT

(TO HIMSELF)I thought that was supposed to be my line…

FAWN
I don't want to go up there again, Kyle! It got too weird last time!

KYLE
We have to check everywhere… You wait here.

FAWN
No! Don't leave me alone!

KYLE
I'll just be a second. We can see the balcony from up there. It'll be quicker than going there! I'll be real quick!

KYLE
Do you want to tell me just what the fuck is going on here, asshole? What's with these stupid games? And where's Indy?

JEVAN
Kyle, where's your ticket? The show's about to start?

KYLE
I said that's enough of the bullshit, Jevan! Let's go!

KYLE
I said 'let's go'!

KYLE (CONT'D)
Fuck!!

FAWN
Where've you been? We've been worried. (SCANNING JEVAN) Are you okay? You look sick.(BEAT) We've got to find Indy, she's missing. Have you seen her?

KYLE

Come on. Let's look in the foyer.

FLETCHER
Hello boys and girls! How're we doing? Who wants a drink? My shout!

RANDALL
(SHORTLY) Good evening, Wayne. Erm, we're fine. Thank you.

.

FLETCHER
Okay. Alright. Well, that's an easy round then, isn't it?

LIZ
God, that man! He is SO uncouth!

DOCTOR NIGHTINGALE
Liz dear, I know he can be a little coarse, but I think he's well intentioned.

RANDALL
And we know what they say about the road to hell though, auntie…

STEWART
(TO RANDAL) You'd know all about that as well, wouldn't you?

RANDALL
I'm sorry, but Liz is right. He drives that awful sports car of his far too fast through the village. And when he walks his dog through the churchyard he lets it… Well, you know.

DOCTOR NIGHTINGALE
I know he might be a little thoughtless, but that doesn't make him a bad person. Always looks below the surface! And I know what I'M talking about!

FLETCHER
So, the lovely Karen up there tells me that you're off tomorrow.

STEWART

Yes. Just having a last minute drink with…

FLETCHER
Well, it's not much of a send-off, is it?

STEWART
I don't like a fuss…

FLETCHER
Please yourself. What do you reckon, Rev? Don't you think he should have has more of a send-off?

RANDALL
It's really none of my business.

FLETCHER
If you ask me, personally, I think he should stay here, mate! (TO STEWART)This is the greatest nation in the world. We've got history! Breeding! Eh?

LIZ
(SARCASTICALLY) Really?
FLETCHER
Well, yeah. We've got thousands of years of history, haven't we? What have the yanks got? A couple of hundred at best. I tell you. No breeding!

DOCTOR NIGHTINGALE
You mean the European influence doesn't go back that far. Native American cultures have a very rich history and they have a good deal of what you call 'breeding'!

FLETCHER
That WAS until we took civilisation to them.

LIZ
I wouldn't call stealing their land and corrupting their culture 'civilising'!

RANDALL
You should read-up on your anthropology, Wayne. Native American oral history and their historic references have every relevance to our own.

FLETCHER

George Washington and George Knox had it right. Manifest Destiny!

LIZ
Do you know that we took Chicken Pox and Measles to the Americas?

RANDALL
Not to mention the Small Pox infected blankets. It was all most regrettable.

FLETCHER
Well, we learn from our mistakes, don't we?

DOCTOR NIGHTINGALE
Do we? How often do the words of George Santayana come into mind? *'Those who cannot remember the past are condemned to repeat it.'*
We've all got our demons, haven't we..?

LIBRARIAN
Sir! Sir! You can't deface those books!

STEWART
Sorry! Sorry! I'll be right back! I'll be right back!

STEWART
Fawn! Fawn! Fawn! It's Mister Stewart!

MATT
That's weird.

WENDY
What is?

MATT
I was here yesterday with Indy and we saw a rat in there so we shut the door to keep it in.

WENDY
So?

MATT

Well the door's open now.

WENDY
You're not scared of rats, are you?

MATT
That's not what I mean. Somebody's obviously been in there. The rats didn't open it themselves.

WENDY
It has to be Jevan or Indy. There was no one in there. You checked.

MATT
There's nothing there now. Let's go.

KYLE
Okay. No more screwing around. We've got to find a way out of here and fast!

FAWN
But what about Indy?

KYLE
There's nowhere else to look! We've been all over!

FAWN
But she HAS to be here.

KYLE
We've looked! She's not on the roof because that's boarded up. She's not in the basement either.

MATT
Anything?

FAWN
You?

MATT
Dude, where've you been? We've been worried. (BEAT) You look awful!

KYLE
Okay, let's go to the stage door and find some way of breaking it down.
MATT
That's a big door!

KYLE
Noted! But unless you've got a better idea that's what we're going to have to do.

MATT
There should still be some tools in the workshop.

KYLE
Yeah, well go look.

FAWN
What if Indy comes back here?

KYLE
You wait here for her.

FAWN
You're nuts if you think I'm staying here on my own!

KYLE
Jevan can stay with you. That way you can make sure he doesn't wander off again…

KYLE (CONT'D)
…because if he does, I swear to God I'm going to pin him down and take a dump on his face.

FAWN
You know, you really DO look sick.

FAWN (CONT'D)
Are you okay? (BEAT) I'll get you some water.

FAWN (CONT'D)
Jesus, Jevan! What's wrong with you!?

FAWN
Indy! Jevan's after me!

KYLE
It's just a bunch of saws and drill bits.

MATT
We need an axe.

KYLE
I know we need an axe!

WENDY
What about where they keep the fire extinguishers? There might be axes in there.

KYLE
Where DO they keep the fire extinguishers?

MATT
There should be some in the hallway. They should be all over.

KYLE
I'm going to tell Fawn and Jev what we're doing and we'll meet at the stage door in ten.

SAUNDERS
Mr Stewart, I really don't know what you expect me to do? If, as you suggest, these youngster are in danger, I suggest you go back to the police and have them force entry. I am not a policeman.

STEWART
But it was the police that sent me to see you!

SAUNDERS
Didn't you explain the situation to them?

STEWART
Yes... but they thought I was some sort of psycho...

SAUNDERS
But you expect ME to believe you? (BEAT) Mr Stewart, you come bursting into my office shouting and screaming about demons, cults and rituals and you expect me to jump right up and help?

STEWART
Just take a look at my notes! Please!

SAUNDERS
Okay, I'll look at your notes but then I want you to leave or I'LL be the one calling the police!

STEWART
It's all true. Trust me.

SAUNDERS
So can you explain to me why six people would be killed every year on this particular date?

STEWART
The village stands above some caves where they used to entomb their... still alive!

SAUNDERS
Go on...

STEWART
There were six of them... Walled-up because the tribe believed them possessed by demons!

SAUNDERS
A fascinating theory Mr Stewart and...

SAUNDERS

(SFX – ECHO) …100% correct.

SAUNDERS
They're just a precaution Mr. Stewart.

SAUNDERS (CONT'D)
It's just Aspirin. I should imagine you have quite a headache.

STEWART
What the hell is this all about?

SAUNDERS
(PONDERINGLY)Hell..? Do you believe in Hell, Mr Stewart? I do. Well, I have to. It's part of the job. It's right up there with seeing the trash is collected and making sure the street lights work.

STEWART
So you know about all this?

SAUNDERS
Know about it..? I administer it. It was a party of Shinnecock who stopped here whilst travelling west. As you say they discovered the catacombs. They awoke some ancient entities who took possession of the first six souls who penetrated the cave. The rest of the tribe of course suspected evil spirits and – for once – primitive superstition and suspicion proved to be absolutely on the money. Those who were possessed were slaughtered but the demons migrated to other members of the party. The survivors somehow managed to lure those possessed into the catacombs and seal them in… still alive. Of course, once they were re-opened…

STEWART
So six people have died EVERY YEAR since then?

SAUNDERS

Yes.

STEWART
But I don't understand why!

SAUNDERS
The legend further continues that if the appetites of the demons could be sated by the sacrifice of six souls every year, they would never emerge and so the mortal world would be safe.

KYLE
Where've you been? We've looked everywhere for you?

STEWART
So six people die every year because of this? That's just insane!

SAUNDERS
Possibly... With this office and all of the other civil services of Amityville, including the Police Department, run by eager disciples it's been relatively easy to maintain, too. We control things in such a way that the dots are never quite joined up... I have to protect the greater good... or, in this case, the greater evil.

STEWART
Surely there's something you can do. With the power of this office..?

STEWART
So innocent souls will continue to be sacrificed in the name of evil?

SAUNDERS
Innocent..? I know all about Miss. Harriman. Her family was far from innocent.

STEWART
What do you mean? I knew the Harrimans well.

SAUNDERS
So did I. The Harrimans were what you might call very 'active' in the community. They were... believers.

STEWART

Believers in what?

SAUNDERS
In what every single inhabitant of Amityville believes in. The sacrifice of their first-born to our demon masters. It's… it's kind of a tradition. When they had the twins they were able to make the ultimate donation.

STEWART
The Harrimans never had tw… Oh Christ!
SAUNDERS
Fawn was the younger twin. Adrienne was twenty minutes older and so, technically, their 'first born'. They were such beautiful babies. Absolutely identical aside from a small birthmark that Adrienne had just below her right ear… But otherwise perfect likenesses of each other.

STEWART
And the fire..?

SAUNDERS
'All must live in the demon's wake,' Mr Stewart. Fawn was saved so we could feed her to the demons themselves. A kind of an apology. The first year the Harrimans didn't take Fawn to the cabin with it was burned and the Harrimans with it. Punishment for their deception.

STEWART
You can't let this go on happening!

SAUNDERS
It'll carry on until it's finished.

STEWART
And when will that be, Mayor?

SAUNDERS
I think tonight.

SAUNDERS
I cannot make amends for the this town's past conformity to evil, but I can try to do something to secure a better future.

STEWART

Thank you.

SAUNDERS
You'd better make haste. Your young charges will need help.

STEWART
You'll have to come with me!

SAUNDERS
No. No. I hold no place in the future. I represent something which is corrupt and vile. I need to break the chain.

STEWART
But I can't get in? I've tried. Remember?

SAUNDERS
This, the Key to the City, has certain… 'properties'. You'll find it'll work in the lock of any door. Go now, and may your efforts mark the beginning of a new and brighter future for this town.

STEWART
Thank you.

SAUNDERS
But remember, saving Fawn and her friends will anger the demons, so you MUST get help. You must get everyone out of that building and ensure no one, NO ONE goes in there.

STEWART
Thank you.

MATT
That's it. Did you find anything in the office?

WENDY
No.

MATT
So there's no axes… but if we find something heavy we can use it as a battering-ram.

WENDY
No, we've got to get back to the stage door. It's probably been ten minutes.

MATT
Alright. Let's go.

MATT
Mr. Stewart?

STEWART
Matt? (BEAT) Where is everyone?

MATT
How did you get in?

STEWART
(INDICATING WENDY) Who's this?

MATT
This is Wendy. She lives here.

STEWART
Explain it to me later. Where is everybody?

MATT
We were just on our way to go meet up with the others. Some pretty strange stuff has been going on.
STEWART
Believe me, I know all about it and it's about to get a whole lot worse. We need to find the other and get out of here right now!

MATT
They're not here. They must still be in the dressing room.

STEWART
Where's that?

MATT
I'll show you.

STEWART

No. No. I'll find it! You'd better get out.

WENDY
That guy back there? Just saved your ass! They have everything they need.

It's a strange thing to say and MATT is nonplussed.

MATT
They..?

WENDY's expression is blank.

WENDY
Just go…

MATT
You coming..?

STEWART
Hello..?

STEWART
Fawn? Fawn? It's Mr. Stewart.

STEWART (CONT'D)
Where is everybody?

'INDY'/'KYLE'/'JEVAN'
You know us, Mr. Stewart. You remember us, don't you, Mr. Stewart? Surely you recognise us, Mr. Stewart.

STEWART
I'm taking Fawn!

'INDY'
Fawn's waiting.

'KYLE'
She's going to help us…

'JEVAN'
To get out.

STEWART
What happened to Indy, Kyle and Jevan?

'INDY'
That's us.

'KYLE'
You know us.

'JEVAN'
From school.

STEWART
You're not them! I know everything. The Mayor told me.

'INDY'
A bargain maker.

'KYLE'
Who makes a bargain.

'JEVAN'
Only in order to break it.

'INDY'
Help us then.
'KYLE'
Three of us here.

'JEVAN'

And three left to sate.

STEWART
You can't leave without the six! The others have gone! There's no one else left.

'INDY'
You're here.

'KYLE'
And Fawn.

'JEVAN'
Who's going to help.

STEWART
But that still only makes five!

STEWART (CONT'D)
Ohhh... Six!

STEWART (CONT'D)
I don't know what else to do!

STEWART (CONT'D)
They've gone!

STEWART
If we run I'm sure we can make it.

STEWART
Fawn?

'FAWN'

It's ADRIENNE!!

END

ABOUT THE AUTHOR

John R Walker works at a BBC daytime drama show as a 1st AD and doesn't get anywhere near the time he wants to make lots of indie films.

His is the director of a film called **Ouijageist** and accidental co-director of a film called **5G zombies**.
He plays a news reporter called **Peter Sommers** in many indie films and lives in Dudley in the UK with Mrs. Walker and their little girl.